W9-BRY-012

MURDER IN MOUNT HOLLY

MURDER IN MOUNT HOLLY

PAUL THEROUX

Mysterious Press
an imprint of Grove/Atlantic, Inc.
New York

Originally published in 1969 in Great Britain by Alan Ross

Published simultaneously in Canada
Printed in the United States of America

ISBN-13: 978-0-8021-2604-7

Mysterious Press
an imprint of Grove/Atlantic, Inc.
841 Broadway
New York, NY 10003

Distributed by Publishers Group West

www.groveatlantic.com

11 12 13 14 15   10 9 8 7 6 5 4 3 2 1

MURDER
IN
MOUNT HOLLY

Prologue

A decent interval after his father died, about a month or so, Herbie Gneiss bought the *Mount Holly Chickadee*, studied the classified ads and said, "Hee-hee-hee."

Late the same evening he picked up the newspaper again, ripped out a little section and laughed again. His laughter came in bursts, like a tire-pump being plunged very quickly.

The next day he stood in a phone booth and dialed a number. Although he frowned several times while he was speaking on the phone, he smiled when he left the booth.

Mr. Gibbon squinted at the grey specks moving toward him. Soon he made out the distinctive shape of a Patton tank leading a convoy of supply trucks. Jeeps loaded with troops followed the trucks. Far behind were the soldiers, thousands of troops wearing field packs, carrying the wounded, staggering, pushing toward Mr. Gibbon who stood at attention in his starched uniform. Far to the rear were the guided missiles on flat-cars, the big bombers overhead, crates and crates of ammo stenciled with the familiar battalion insignia (a jackdaw with a worm in its beak; the motto *Pro Futuro Aedificamus*). Mr. Gibbon's heart skipped slightly as he raised his hand and waved the convoy past him. He saluted the big brass in the jeeps, the old man himself, tough, steely, sitting there with a bottle of bourbon clenched between his knees. He nodded to the foot soldiers.

Everything was okay.

"Roger," said Mr. Gibbon. He licked his pencil and made a notation on a clipboard.

In the cloakroom of the Mount Holly Kindergarten Miss Ball counted coins from a jam jar into a dark hand. When she had counted all the coins she gestured for them to be put back into the jar. The counting started again.

The coins had been counted four times when Miss Ball turned the jam jar over and tapped on the bottom. Then she shook it. There was no sound.

The dark hand closed on the coins.

"Mucho, mucho," Miss Ball said. Then she said, "Better hurry off pronto."

Part One

1

Herbie had no choice. He had to get a job, for his mother's sake anyway. They weren't dirt-poor and chewing their nails, but his father's death insurance did not cover everything. At his mother's request he had to quit college and come home. His mother now thought she would starve. Herbie would have to work to support his mother; she was a very fat lady.

"I eat like a bird, but everything I eat turns to fat," was Mrs. Gneiss's explanation as she stared wide-eyed at her enormous knees.

Herbie imagined everything she ate adhering to the inside of her skin, inflating her. Nothing ever left his mother's body. Everything stuck.

"I've raised you good," she would say in her suety voice, her lips never touching. "And I think it's high time you made things a little easier for me. I haven't got long and I want it to be sweet."

Herbie had entered college happily. He had been told dozens of times that he was not, as they say, "college material," but from what he could gather neither were any of the other 30,000 students. And if they were, and if the cross notes from the professors had any truth in them, then (*a*) it either took a long time to find the slobs, separate the wheat from the chaff or (*b*) any college worth its salt could tolerate a few ignoramuses or, as Herbie pictured himself, late-bloomers. He had planned on staying.

Once when he went home—it was Easter—he noticed that his father's processes seemed to be slowing down. A visit home after being away for more than a month made it clear to him that his father was slowly dying. Things were stopping in him, like lights being switched off in different parts of a city as you watch from a hill.

When Herbie got the news that it was all over he stomped his new wastebasket flat. Then he went home, rented a black suit, went to his father's funeral, was consoled by some people he didn't know, and before he knew it was back at college.

Almost as soon as he got off the bus after returning to college Herbie had trouble calling up the image of his father's face. He wished that his father had had a craggy face, an awful grin or a bald head, if only to remember him by. But Herbie could not remember what his father looked like. His father had no evidence of his having passed through and on, no evidence except some unpaid bills in

4

the bottom bureau drawer and a bowling ball in the closet with undersized finger holes. It was his father's pride and joy. He had it specially made for his small hands. Mrs. Gneiss discovered to her horror that, because of the holes, it was nearly unpawnable.

Fearing the worst, death by starvation, Mrs. Gneiss ate everything there was to eat in the house the evening Mr. Gneiss died. For a month this went on. She ran up bills and stocked the house with food, bought more and ran up more bills. Any hour of the day Mrs. Gneiss could be seen in front of the television set licking her fingers.

One day Herbie got the letter he had been expecting:

Dear Herbert,

I think it's finally coming. Death, I mean. But that's okay. You go on with your studies and you study hard like you always meant to and someday you'll know what it's like to be a parent who is dying and has only a few moments to live (I wonder if I'll even have time to sign this letter?????). You be an awfully good boy and "brace up" and remember to send your kids to college like I worked and slaved to. Teach them never to be "ungrateful" and "smart-alecky" and not to smoke in bed. I better stop now because my eyes are all sandy and tearing from crying and I need

more light. Guess this is it. Oops, another pain.
In the chest this time. Hope you're getting all "A's"
in all your subjects. Guess this is "Goodbye" like
they say. If you need anything just ask for it. I'll
be glad to do anything you want for you. You only
have to ask, I'm always here.

So long from,
Your Sick "Mom"

He left the next day. When he arrived home his mother
met him on the porch. She greeted him with a heavy and
prolonged belch. She thumped her chest and reminded
Herbie that that's where the pains were. Right (urp) there.

"Hello, Ma."

"I'm dying, Herbie."

"I know."

"This time it's for real."

"I got your letter."

Mrs. Gneiss returned to where she had been sitting.
A bowl of ice cream, half-full, rested on the coffee table.
Nearby there was a bag of potato chips. Mrs. Gneiss cradled
the bowl in her lap and picked up the potato chip bag
and placed it next to her on the sofa. Then she dunked a
potato chip into the ice cream, scooped up some ice cream
and tossed the whole mess into her mouth. She licked and
chewed and waited for Herbie to speak.

Herbie couldn't think of anything to say.

"A mother's got rights," Mrs. Gneiss said thickly. Her next potato chip scoop broke under the strain of so much ice cream. "What ever happened to those man-sized chips?" she asked, glancing around the room.

"What do you want me to do?"

"You see any?"

"Any what?"

"Man-sized chips for the ice-cream dip."

Herbie stood up and went to the far corner of the room. Then, at a safe distance, he shouted: "Look, I don't mind getting your lousy letters and I don't mind coming back to this stinking house, but I do mind leaving college for good, moving out of the dorm, selling my bike . . ."

"Your gorgeous bike," Herbie's mother mocked.

". . . I said to myself, What's a semester? I said to myself . . ."

"You're going to give your mother a semester to die in?"

". . . I thought you were lonely. I thought you needed someone around the house. I thought you were in trouble, sick or something . . ."

"I *am* sick."

"You don't look sick to me."

"The sickest people in the world don't look sick. I'm sick at heart. Heart-sick, that's what I am. And afraid."

"You said you were *dying* in the letter."

"Of course I'm dying. What do you expect? You think I'm going to live forever?"

"I mean now. You said you were dying now."

"You mean this semester?" Mrs. Gneiss chewed.

"I don't know what I mean. I only thought that it was urgent. Now I get here and it doesn't look so urgent."

Mrs. Gneiss continued mumbling: "I wouldn't have gotten you away from your precious books if I didn't think it was urgent," she finished quickly. "Now I'm sick and that's all there is to it."

Herbie started to say something.

"I know what you're going to say. *You don't look sick.* [She mimicked him perfectly.] Well, for your information, I *am* sick. Seriously ill, as they say. I say I'm sick, and if I say I'm sick that should be good enough for you. If it's not . . ." Mrs. Gneiss thought a moment. "If it's not, well, tough taffy, you're home and you're staying home until I drop. You've got to like it or lump it. You've got to *learn* to like it—as we used to say back at *college!*" This sent Mrs. Gneiss into torrents of creamy laughter.

With only his mother's death on his mind, Herbie said, "Okay."

"It won't be so bad."

"No."

"Of course, you might have to get a job, and all that."

A *job?* The word had almost no meaning for Herbie. He was one of those people who had escaped the tedium of paper routes and had dodged what other more enterprising adolescents had got: selling glow-in-the-dark Krismiss Kards, foot balm, tins of greasy unguent—all in return for B-B guns and autographed catchers' mitts. Herbie had never worked a day in his life. There was simply no need to work. He liked to read and had started smoking at an early age. So why should he have had to work (of all things) to kill time? There were thousands of ways to kill time without working. And besides, his father was always there, *had been* at least. A very little man, very generous, very hard to remember; one of those faces that no one can describe—probably a perfect criminal's face. Herbie had gotten money out of him. Now Herbie missed him, for the first time in his life.

Herbie sighed.

"It won't be for long," said Herbie's mother. Then she added, "Although the longer the better, if you can see this from my point of view."

Herbie looked at his mother. She was still eating away happily, shoveling in the ice cream on potato chips. One thing about his mother: she wasn't a show off. She didn't try to pretend she was thin. She knew she was fat. She looked fat. She had no time for girdles; she never used make-up, had never had her face lifted. Her one extravagance had been painting her toenails, but this was now virtually impossible.

9

She would have had to learn to be a contortionist, and she knew there were no fat contortionists. Her wish now was to sit, to be left alone with a lot of food, and to spread in all directions under her kimono. There are two ways to die, Herbie thought: one, you don't eat enough and you starve to death; two, you stuff yourself and collapse with a belch. No, he didn't hate her. But if she had to go it might as well happen along the starchy street she had been traveling all along. It was her wish.

"When do I start?"

"Very soon."

"All right, I'll just unpack . . ."

"Don't bother," said Herbie's mother.

"Don't bother? I thought you said you wanted me around?"

"I do," she said, shushing him. "I want you around here so bad I could yell, but there are no jobs hereabouts, so you'll have to live near where you work . . ."

Herbie's mother summed up the job situation. There were too many Puerto Ricans from God knows where working for a song. They took all the jobs there were to take. It was the way of these Puerto Rican people. They really didn't want the jobs. What they really wanted was a lot of bananas. But their senses told them: move in and take the jobs. They didn't know what to do with the jobs once they got them, but there were a lot of Puerto Ricans and only a few good honest hardworking kids like Herbie in Holly Heights.

Holly Heights was a suburb of Holly. There were also Lower Holly, Mount Holly, Holly-on-the-Ivy (a creek), East, West, North and South Holly, Holly Junction, Holly Falls, Holly Rapids, Hollyville, Hollypool, Hollyminster, Holly Springs and a dozen others, including, yes, Hollywood. This covered an area of about two hundred square miles.

If Herbie moved into Holly proper, or in the adjoining burg of Mount Holly, he would have a better chance. There were lots of jobs going begging.

"I've never begged in my life," said Herbie.

"Oh, tons of jobs," Herbie's mother said. "Just remember, there are bills to pay. Medicine, your father's medicine. It seems a downright shame to have to pay for medicine now that he's dead. It seems crazy. I mean, why did we buy the medicine in the first place? And the embalmer's fees, the flowers and the headstone. Well, that's a break—you won't have to get another headstone for me, although you'll have to have my name chiseled on the stone. Extra with the initial. And there's always my food. Food is just like medicine to me." Mrs. Gneiss stopped talking as soon as she remembered what she had said about her dead husband's medicine.

"A job."

"When we get some cash you'll be free and clear. So will I. I'll be able to rest easy." *Rest easy*, Mrs. Gneiss thought; that's a slip of the tongue. "Just try not to think about it," she went on. "Do your work and send home some cash every week. I'll send you fried chicken in the mail, and letters too. Like always." Then, for no reason at all, she said, "It'll be like old times."

"I was doing pretty good at college, you know."

"You'll be able to go back," said Herbie's mother. "After."

"Mmmm."

"Do this for me, Herbie. Just this once."

Herbie promised that he would. His mother really wasn't so bad. Just fat was all. He would go to Mount Holly and make good. There were lots of jobs there; lots of factories were crying to get people.

"Kant-Brake," said Herbie's mother. "They need people real bad."

"Well, maybe I'll look them up."

"You will."

"I will?"

"Yes, I've written a letter to the owner. Used to know your father," said Mrs. Gneiss, handing her son the letter. "You've just got to look neat as a pin and they'll hire you. And give them the letter."

"What the hell," Herbie said. "Might as well be there as any other place. What did you say they made there?"

"Toys. You know, toys? Those little . . ."

"Oh, toys."

Mrs. Gneiss was through with her explanation. She turned back to the TV. She champed her ice cream sullenly. After a few moments a fearful burp trembled through her body, crinkling her kimono and making her shake her head. It sent Herbie out of the room and into bed.

The next day Herbie kissed his mother goodbye and took the bus to Holly Heights. When he arrived he bought a newspaper. First a room, then a job, he thought. His eye was caught by an ad for a room. He called the number. A woman answered and, though her voice was a trifle shrill, seemed nice. She said he'd have to come over. Herbie agreed. Herbie mentioned Kant-Brake Toys. She said she had another boarder at Kant-Brake Toys. Herbie said that sounded just fine. He went right over.

2

Mr. Gibbon was a fuddy-duddy, not a geezer, but he was old, chewed his lips, dressed horribly and so often he was taken for a geezer. He lived in Miss Ball's house on the second floor.

He had few possessions. Each possession had a special significance. There was his comb. It was *part* of a comb, about five plastic teeth at various distances apart on a bitten spine. Mr. Gibbon had used that same comb since boot camp. It was the last thing his aunt gave him. In fact, it was the last thing his aunt gave anybody, since she died on the railroad platform waving goodbye to the seventeen-year-old Charlie Gibbon as his train pulled away bound for New Jersey. So the comb was special. He used the comb often. The strange and even sick part of it all was that he used it without a mirror. He would stand, one arm crooked over his head; his eyes on an object so distant that it had no name, and he would scrape away at his scalp with those five plastic teeth.

Like most old men he wore his watch to bed. He had forgotten the last time it was off his wrist. But he remembered distinctly the time he got it, a bargain at the Fort Sam Baker PX in Missouri, two dollars and sixty cents. It was a huge watch and ticked very loudly. The chrome had flaked off and revealed brass underneath. The watch was so big that even Mr. Gibbon could wind it. And Mr. Gibbon had very thick fingers.

Mr. Gibbon's other valuable possessions were his .45 caliber pistol (he had killed a man with it, he said), his canteen with the bullet hole through the side (it had foiled the killing of Mr. Gibbon), a picture of his wife and two daughters in a bamboo frame he had bought somewhere near the equator somewhere on an island somewhere, also his army discharge papers, his khakis, his clips of bullets, his hunting knife ("A man should own enough knife to protect himself with," he said), his neatly made bed, his paper bags and his tennis shoes.

Of these last two items the bags were the most important; the tennis shoes were more of a sentimental thing. Mr. Gibbon made it a practice to carry paper bags wherever he went, wrinkled brown-paper bags. It was hard to tell what was in the bags since they were not bulky enough to show the outlines of any distinguishable object. Even if they did contain a large object they were wrinkled enough to conceal the object's identity. Often the paper bags contained nothing more than many carefully folded paper bags. Mr. Gibbon enjoyed the stares of people who were perplexed by a particularly huge brown-paper bag he had carried into town one day. He did not take the bus that day. Instead he walked all the way home, past all the eyes of most of his neighbors. What was in the bag? More bags. Mr. Gibbon smiled and tucked his secret under his arm. Many times he hailed and hooted a good morning to another old man merely because the other man was also carrying a bag. He imagined a fraternity of old men carrying armloads of wrinkled bags. He saw them all the time.

The tennis shoes replaced his army boots, which he saved for special occasions (riding in a car, resting, cleaning his pistol). They were black basketball sneakers—the kind that a high school student wears after school. The canvas was black, the rubber was white. In spite of the thick rubber soles they added no spring to his step. He walked along the sidewalk with a pflap-pflip-pflap-pflip of the canvas and rubber, the long lacings trailing several inches behind. Over the anklebone there was a round label which read:

OFFICIAL TENNIES
"The Choice of Major Leaguers!"

He wore no socks. Usually his trousers were baggy and long enough to conceal the fact, but sometimes his white ankle flesh could be seen over the black tennis shoes as he walked along the sidewalk looking very much like a little wooden man marching down a plank, weaving from side to side.

What nearly everyone noticed first about Mr. Gibbon were his eyes. They were cloudy, pearly and ill-looking. It was his eyes that got him discharged from the army and not the fact that he was at retirement age. He had changed his age several times on his file card to make absolutely sure that he would die in the army. There was no way to disperse the fog in his eyes. He could see all right, his eyes were "damn good" and he had never been sick a day in his life. Yet his eyes looked wrong. They were the wrong color. Indeed, there seemed to be something seriously wrong with those eyes. They were the color of nonfat milk.

Mr. Gibbon's nose was sharp, as was his chin and the ridge of his head where the skull sutures pushed against the skin. His neck was a collection of wattles, folds and very thin wrinkles. The base of his neck seemed small, bird-like, as if it had been choked thin by a tight collar for many years.

And his mouth. "I've got fifteen teeth," Mr. Gibbon was fond of saying. The teeth were not visible. They were somewhere within the shapeless lips, which stretched and chewed even when Mr. Gibbon was not eating. It was the kind of mouth that caused people to think that he was a nasty man.

From the rear he looked like nearly every other man his age. His head was wide at the top, not a dome, but a wedge. The back of his skinny neck was an old unhappy face of wrinkles. There was even a wrinkle the size of a small mouth, frowning from the back of Mr. Gibbon's neck. His ears stuck out, his shoulders were bony and rounded, his spine protruded. He was vaguely bucket-assed, but not so much bucket-like as edgy, a flat bottom that is known as starchy, as if it contained a large piece of cardboard.

"You can't rile me," Mr. Gibbon said. It was mostly true. He stayed calm most of the time, and when he was angry did not speak: instead he wheezed, he puffed, he blew, he sighed, he groaned. And maybe he would mumble an obscenity or two.

His favorite song was the National Anthem, and the less violins, the more brass, the better. An old song, he said, but a good solid one. You'd be proud to get up on your hind legs and be counted when it played—it was that kind of song, a patriotic song. "If you wanna name names, I'm a patriot," said Mr. Gibbon. He liked the anonymity of citizenship and patriotism. He wanted to be in that great bunch of great people that listened, that saluted, that obeyed the country's command whether at home or abroad, whether down at the pool hall or far afield, at work or at play. The song ran through him and charged his whole body and made it tingle. Mr. Gibbon wheezed and spat when he was angry, but he also wheezed and spat when he was emotionally involved; he got choked up. Something of a patriotic nature always brought rheum to his eyes: hearing the anthem, seeing the flag or his army buddies. Or just the thought of them.

He had resigned himself to being out of the army as much as he could. You couldn't do it completely. He knew that. It was in the blood. It was something that wouldn't leave you for all your born days. Something you wouldn't want to leave even if it were possible. Something great and good. Something powerful.

It was a sad day when the army doctor took a last look at Mr. Gibbon's cloudy eyes and said, "There's something sick about them eyes. I don't know what medical science would say, but I don't like the looks of them . . ."

That was all there was to it. In a few days Mr. Gibbon was out of the army. He had been in for thirty-eight years. "That's a lifetime for some people, thirty-eight years," he would say. And when he was feeling very low he would say, "That was my lifetime, thirty-eight years in Uncle Sam's army. Just hanging on now for dear life, and I don't know whether I'm coming or going."

Mr. Gibbon was smart enough to know that things were different in the army. Life was better, if not richer. There was good company, a nice bunch of kids. Raw kids, greenhorns, but they learned in the long run. They learned to pitch-in and fall-to. Life in the army was a constant reward. It was Mr. Gibbon's first real haircut, grammar school, a trip to the zoo. For a man who had never had a youth that he remembered, and who could not remember whether (or not) he had passed through puberty, the army was a tremendously satisfying experience. Not really the romance of the recruiting poster, although there was more of that in it than people ordinarily thought. In the army you were someone, a man in khakis, a full-time threat to the enemy; Mr. Gibbon was "Pop" to a lot of young kids and a buddy to a lot of the others. Need a little advice on VD, a needle and thread, some notepaper, card tricks, funny stories? Want to know what the Jerries were really like? Ask Pop Gibbon.

Now he was out of the army and it pained. Maybe it was the weather, but the weather had never caused him to pain before. Pain in his back, his neck, his finger joints. Or his clothes were damp. His clothes had never been damp before. And when he did not pain he felt sticky, or maybe one of his teeth would be giving him a time. In the army he never had a sick day, although the Doc and others examined his eyes now and then and prescribed "rest, lots and lots of rest for them eyes," or "try a little epsom salts, Charlie, bathe them and then get some rest, lots of . . ." Worse than all the civilian aches and pains was the one thought that occurred to him over and over again, the thought which zipped into his mind one morning and which stayed there, for good it seemed. Mr. Gibbon had been on his way to take a bath and did not feel a need to take the precaution of wearing a robe (besides, nakedness always reminded Mr. Gibbon pleasantly of the army). He was padding along the hall placidly, with a towel over his arm and his comb in his hand, and wearing his tennis shoes for slippers, and he passed one of the bedrooms and caught a glimpse of someone moving. He stopped and peeked through the door. He was right. In the full-length mirror he saw an old man, almost totally bald, carrying a broken comb and a tattered towel and wearing a suit of shrivelled fat.

It brought Mr. Gibbon up short. He tried to cover himself with the towel, but to no avail. The towel was too small and too shredded. Mr. Gibbon spilled over into the mirror. When he turned away from the mirror he got the most revolting view of all, a rear view, dying flesh retreating, and it was not starchy at all. It was just awful.

He could not forget the old man in the fat suit walking stupidly, awkwardly away from the full-length mirror. It had not been like that in the army. He had been a big strong man in the army. The army had promised to train Mr. Gibbon. They had kept their promise. They had trained him to check the firing pins on various large caliber shells; they had trained him to cook boiled cabbage and greens for upwards of three hundred hungry, dog-faced foot soldiers; they taught him to weld canteens, shout marching orders, cure rot, detect clap, and execute a nearly perfect about-face. These trades had kept Mr. Gibbon wise, his muscles in tune. In his thirty-eight army years Mr. Gibbon learned many trades up and down.

When he was discharged he found that army trades were not exactly civilian trades, although there were some similarities.

At first Mr. Gibbon did not try to get a job, but as he said, he had always been "on the go." It was the army's way to be always on the go. So twiddling his thumbs did not appeal to him. He was not a man of leisure. He took pride in making and doing a little each day. He had some money and a little pension, but it was not a question of money. Raising chickens was out, so was drinking coffee with unshaven men in the Automat, watching people go by, remembering number plates, spotting cars and playing cards. Mr. Gibbon was a little foolish, but he was not stupid and, perhaps worst of all, he had not yet been blessed with the time-consuming affliction of senility. He was in the still-awake period of dusk, which exists for old people in retirement between the last job and the first trembling signals of crotchety old age and near madness. Still lucid.

He could be useful. To himself and his country. But he was worried when he thought of his training; the army had trained him well, but what use is a firing-pin fixer, rot curer, cabbage boiler and canteen welder in the civilian world? What good? No good, Mr. Gibbon concluded. He took odd jobs at first, and even saw the humor in this. Gibbon, the taker of odd jobs. That's what it had come to.

His first odd job was with the Municipal Council of Lower Holly, directing a road-fixing crew. But the workers would not be threatened with demerits and they did not have the respect (and fear) that recruits generally had for Mr. Gibbon. If Mr. Gibbon gave an order they paused, shuffled their feet, and from the middle of the group of workers another order would be shouted back: "Go back to the old folks' home, Grandpa!" Once a man told him to go suck his thumb.

His next jobs were as an usher at the movies, a special policeman at the Holly Junction bathing beach and as a cabdriver on the late shift of the We-Drive-U-Kwik Cab Company. It was not long before Mr. Gibbon retired his flashlight and braided usher's cap, his badge and nightstick. The odd job with the cab company bore some fruit, killed some time, and it even showed signs of speeding Mr. Gibbon right into his grave with no stopover at senility or madness.

It was his third week on the job that finished him. The week of the teeth. Mr. Gibbon had just gotten an upper plate of new false teeth.

"New false teeth," Mr. Gibbon had said to the dispatcher. "*New* false teeth. False and new. It sounds crazy, doesn't it?"

The cab dispatcher said that he had known a lot of people that had new false teeth. They liked them, the new false teeth. So why should Mr. Gibbon think they were so crazy?

"I didn't say I *thought* they were crazy," Mr. Gibbon corrected. "I said new false teeth *sounded* crazy. Like new used cars sounds crazy."

The cab dispatcher did not see Mr. Gibbon's point at all.

The teeth, both new and false, did not fit well. Or maybe it was Mr. Gibbon's gums that did not fit. Whatever it was, it made his mouth sore, and Mr. Gibbon said he'd have to get his gums in shape before he could stand them a full day. It was toward the end of the third week that the accident happened. The teeth were resting on the seat beside Mr. Gibbon as he drove down Main Street late one night. Then he heard the familiar squawk from the sidewalk and whipped the cab over to the customer. The customer got in and sat on the front seat; Mr. Gibbon said, "Where to, Johnny?"

But when he said it he realized that his teeth were under the man. He reached for them. The man, far from indignant, took Mr. Gibbon's arm and happily guided it. The two-way radio crackled. Mr. Gibbon gasped and struggled with the giggling man for full possession of his hand, his teeth, his wits. The car veered sharply and tore down the

25

wrong lane of Holly Boulevard with the two reaching men, one grasping and wheezing, one delighted, in the front seat. The cab dispatcher back at the We-Drive-U-Kwik office listened to the wheezing and giggling. The cab dispatcher yelled into the microphone. Mr. Gibbon lunged for the radio. In doing so he lost control of the car completely and rammed a utility pole. Two voices—one from the radio, one from the seat next to him—sassed him, told him he was a useless old fool, a flop, and a tease.

The door slammed and the radio went dead. Mr. Gibbon left the We-Drive-U-Kwik Cab Company that same night. His sat-on teeth were broken, his pride had been toyed with, his age mocked once again, and for the first time in his life Mr. Gibbon had been chewed out. In a matter of minutes his job was taken from him. And it was a long time before he found another one.

Six months later Mr. Gibbon became a quality control inspector in the military department of the Kant-Brake Toy Factory. And, like all the other workers in the same department, he wore a uniform showing his rank and months of service. Medals were given for safety, punctuality, and high bowling scores. Mr. Gibbon was in heaven.

It was the logical place to go, but somehow the thought had not even occurred to Mr. Gibbon. Why not a toy factory? It was the only place outside of the army itself that made murderous weapons a speciality. Kant-Brake manufactured soldiers, millions of planes, gunboats, bombers, bullets, sub-machine guns, tents, tanks, Jeeps, and even little officer's quarters right down, as the catalogue said, "to the geraniums on the general's lawn." Every weapon of war, murder, spying or sabotage could be found under the Kant-Brake roof. Some designs, which were under construction, had only just appeared on the drawing boards in the Pentagon. The Kant-Brake Company bragged that it turned out more planes, more ships, and more tanks "than all the world's man-sized factories put together!" They made a nuclear sub that could fire sixteen high-powered missiles. The missiles alone that appeared at Kant-Brake were so many that they were equal in number "to all the bombs dropped by both sides during World War II."

The emphasis was on realism, on craftsmanship. Now the toy soldiers could be wounded, bandaged, cared for. "They bleed real blood!" the ads ran. And everything they said was true—you could hardly tell it from the "real thing." Each item was perfectly formed, expertly detailed; the colonels frowned, the captains were grim, the faces of the foot soldiers were twisted in fear, pain, anxiety. Midget canteens held real water. The bombs fumed, the tanks groaned, the rockets were guaranteed to light up any child's playroom in a red glare.

Mr. Gibbon was good with his hands, and his memory for army details was infallible. He could spot an imperfect

M-1 several feet away. He studied rocketry in the evenings, and he had plans for complicated war games that he hoped would be accepted by the Games Department. Kids nowadays, he said, didn't give a hoot for Chinese Checkers and Old Maid. Kids had a vital interest in the world. War toys stimulated kids to keep up with current events. War toys were good for kids; a well-armed kid could work out all his aggressions in a single Christmas morning.

The director of Kant-Brake also held surprise inspections. The company picnics were called "maneuvers." The annual convention in West Holly was called a "bivouac." The company prospered.

Mr. Gibbon stood at attention near the conveyor belt and squinted at the grey specks moving toward him. As they passed he gave a snappy salute, made a notation on his clipboard and said "Roger." Mr. Gibbon watched the parade of toys pass.

3

Miss Ball taught kindergarten, loved her country and things with catchy names. Her house was full of things with catchy names: Stay-Kleen, Brasso, Reck-Itch, Keentone, Kem-Thrill, Kwickee-Treets and Frosty-Smaks. At school she had Ed-U-Kards in her Ed-U-Kit, Erase-Eez and all the Skool-Way products. She also had a Snooz-Alarm Clock (". . . It lets you sleep") and hundreds of other things with catchy names. They kept her in the swim, she said.

She knew the value of a dollar, and even though she always bought things "on time" she paid her bills. It was not that she owed no man. She owed everyone. But she always paid up.

And so when her lover, Juan, the school janitor, needed a few extra two-bits, she always paid. She called it "pin-money." Juan's demands became more and more, and still Miss Ball paid or promised to pay. She had no intention of dropping Juan just because there wasn't enough money in the jam jar. When Juan grew impatient and muttered in the broom closet, Miss Ball had the presence of mind to take a day off from school.

It took a whole afternoon in the wing chair to come up with the solution. When it finally occurred to her she jumped up from the chair, said "Happy days," and then smugly announced: "I'll advertise."

She did just that. She had plenty of room in the house. Why not take in another boarder? She decided to place an ad in the *Mount Holly Chickadee*. Her ad in the classified section of the paper was characteristic of her sweet disposition.

COMFY ROOM FOR PEANUTS
Large homey room, warm, for single male, hooked rug, big quilt, just perfect for student who wants all the comforts and doesn't mind sharing "boy's room." Kitchen priv., tender loving care. Can't miss. Cheap. Nice. Call after 6. Tel. 65355.

She just couldn't keep it down to twenty-five words. It would have been a crying shame to do that.

She knew that it would click, too. Just as the ad which had fascinated Mr. Gibbon had clicked. But still she ran the ad for three days "just," as she said to Mr. Gibbon, "for the sheer heck of it."

Mr. Gibbon grunted something in return (he was out of sorts) and went on with his paper bags. He was now used to Miss Ball, and on top of it had been in the army. Miss Ball's fling with Juan came as no great surprise. Things like that happened every day when you were in the army. Like when you find out your best buddy is a crumby stooge, or the C. O. is a pansy, or your best girl ran off with your best friend and never wrote back except to say, Dearest, I'm going to make a clean breast of it. It was all in the army, all in the game. As for Miss Ball and Juan, that dago bastard, Mr. Gibbon really didn't give a rat's ass what happened.

He knew that she, Miss Ball, had just had that thing, that operation that women had sometimes. He couldn't blame her. Women always did screwy things like making their hair navy blue (Miss Ball's was "Starry Silver"), or putting lard on their faces, or even running off with the crazy Puerto Rican janitor at the school. He was an army man through and through, and understood these things like other people couldn't understand them, since they had never had the privilege of going out and fighting, really fighting, with their guts, for their country. How could they know? But Mr. Gibbon knew damn well what was going on in Miss Ball's mind. She was having her fling. He had seen a lot of folks come over the hill in his time, a damn sight more than a lot of people he knew that were always shooting their mouths off about human nature and such and such. He had seen people lose their marbles, too. Right in the same foxhole Mr. Gibbon had seen a man lose nearly every one of his marbles. But Mr. Gibbon had not done a damn thing because he had seen a lot of people come over the hill. He had seen guys on leave. Guys that had been in the trenches for days, months even. They had to get it out of their system.

Miss Ball? She had to get it out of her system too. So what if she was near sixty? Did that mean she didn't have anything in her system maybe? Like hell. Gibbon could testify to the exact opposite of that little theory. You could bet your furlough on that. What made people think that young folks were different from old folks? That was something Mr. Gibbon could not understand.

What went for Mr. Gibbon went for Miss Ball. They were friends, comrades. Mr. Gibbon said nothing and that was good enough for Miss Ball. If Mr. Gibbon had told her one time he had told her a hundred: *You're young at heart.*

"You're young *too*," Miss Ball cheeped, when Mr. Gibbon gave his consent to the unsavory business with Juan.

"Not me, Toots," Mr. Gibbon said gruffly.

Miss Ball had said he could have it his way. And he did have it his way. He could see what was going on in Miss Ball's head, thinking all those crazy things. But still, he knew she was in no danger. It was her way. She *was* young at heart; why else did she stay up late reading all those movie magazines? But you'd never catch Mr. Gibbon making a damn fool out of himself with any two-bit big-assed movie queen (both Miss Ball and the magazines called them "starlets").

Miss Ball believed that she was a starlet, although a little older than most of the other starlets. After her hysterectomy she believed it even more. And that was when Juan came onstage and left his broom behind. A few months later she placed the ad. It was all nice.

The ad clicked, as Miss Ball had predicted, to Mr. Gibbon.

After one day the phone rang.

The voice was young. A young gentleman. Perfect.

"Herbie what?" Miss Ball asked.

"Gneiss," said Herbie. He spelled it out and then pronounced it.

This bewildered Miss Ball. She asked him his nationality.

"American, I guess."

"You guess?"

"American."

"We're all Americans in this house," said Miss Ball triumphantly. "Me and Mr. Gibbon—he's the most American one of all. You'll like him lots."

"I'm sure I will," said Herbie.

Herbie went on to inquire about the "boy's room" that was mentioned in the ad. What exactly was the boy's room and who would he have to share it with?

"I should have explained," said Miss Ball. "I'm a *teacher*. I teach kindergarten in the basement of Mount Holly High. We call the boy's room the boy's room. I should have explained. How silly of me!" She giggled.

"Oh," said Herbie.

"What do you do?"

"Well, I'm not working at present. But I think I'll be working at Kant-Brake. The toy factory."

"Holy mackerel! That's where Mr. Gibbon works! What a co-*in*-cidence!"

"Fabulous," said Herbie dryly.

"Why, you can't turn me down *now*!" Miss Ball said with glee. "Mr. Gibbon'll be sore as a boil if you don't come."

"I see," said Herbie.

"We've got something in *com*-mon!" exclaimed Miss Ball as if she had found her son, lost these many years.

"So we do," said Herbie.

34

"I'll expect you for supper. At six. Don't be a minute late, Mr. Gibbon doesn't like cold greens."

"Who is this Mr. Gibbon?" Herbie asked. But Miss Ball had already hung up.

A new tenant! It was like a gift from above. *He will provide.* That was Miss Ball's motto. He always provided. First the operation, then Juan, then Herbie, who worked at the very same place as Mr. Gibbon! Wonders never did cease as long as He provided in the moment of need. He could positively move mountains. Good Old Providence.

In Miss Ball's case He had moved something considerably more spherical than a mountain. He did just that from His Dwelling Place Up There where things were white mostly, soft, and didn't cost a cent. It really was as simple as all that. If only people knew what the very simple secret was: make yourself like a little child. You had to make yourself tiny and really believe in that Big Man Up There. Making herself like a starlet was, in her mind, the same thing as making herself like a little child, pleasing and fresh as a daisy to The Big Fellow In The Sky. And why not a starlet? Especially since she had a natural bent in that direction, a gift, so to speak. It was all the same. He knew what was in your heart. You couldn't fool Him.

So Miss Ball got a new tenant, Herbie, and she was able to raise Juan's allowance, and she found that she was better natured to her kindergarten. Everything was rosy. All the money that Herbie would pay for room and board Miss Ball would turn over to Juan. It all came out in the end. She was no Jew. Why should she try to make a buck on a kid that didn't have beans to start with? That wasn't her way. Not Miss Ball. Maybe *some* people, but not Miss Ball.

4

"So what, he's nice," Mr. Gibbon said. Herbie had not come at six. Mr. Gibbon had his cold greens and grumbled about them, and now, at breakfast, he was still grumbling. Herbie had arrived late and Mr. Gibbon had heard the racket. He was awakened from a vicious dream: a Dark Stranger was trying to steal his paper bags. The Dark Stranger had snatched nearly every one of them. It was a Negro, a tall one, who wanted the bags to put watermelons in. Mr. Gibbon had fought with him, and during the fight woke to the noise of Herbie banging the bureau drawers in the next room.

"That's his name." Miss Ball spelled it out and pronounced it. "Gneiss."

"It sounds Jewish if you ask me."

"Everything sounds Jewish if you say it a certain way," said Miss Ball, trying for a little wisdom. "But he's not. He's not Jewish."

"Probably changed it."

"He said he's American."

"All Jews think they're Americans. Everybody does. That's the only fault I can find with this country. Everybody thinks they're so damn big. Like this Gneiss."

"Don't be so cranky. You don't even know him."

"You're the one who's cranky."

"He's okay. He looks tip-top. Very clean-looking."

"That's not like you, Miss Ball. Sticking up for a Jew."

"I'm not sticking up for a Jew. I'm sticking up for my new boarder."

"He's a Jew."

"He's not. He's a fine young man with a remarkably small nose."

"What's the difference. They'll take over the country, like everyone else, I suppose. They'll come." Mr. Gibbon heaved a sigh. "But I hope to God they don't come in my lifetime."

"Shush," said Miss Ball. "You're big and strong. You've got a lot of time left."

"I hate that expression *you've got a lot of time left*. Like you're waiting to punch the time clock and drop dead."

"He must be dead tired. He came by bus all the way from Holly Heights."

"Used to have a guy in the platoon named Gnefsky, or something like that. He was a Jew."

"He's not a Jew."

"Don't tell me! He was in my platoon, not yours. I should know."

"I mean Herbie, the new boy."

Mr. Gibbon muttered. He couldn't grit his teeth. He didn't have enough of them to grit.

"He wanted to know what the boy's room was. Isn't that *precious?*"

"In the army we used to call it the crapper. He probably doesn't know what *that* means either."

"Now you just be careful what you say," said Miss Ball. She clapped her hands and then said, "Oh, I'm so excited! It's like opening night!"

"He probably smokes in bed."

"It reminds me of the day I saw the playback of my movie. That was in . . . let's see . . ."

For, the next few minutes Miss Ball relived a story she had told so many times that Mr. Gibbon was actually interested to see what changes she had made since the last time he heard it. There she was, Miss Ball in her first starring role, madly in love with the dashing special agent. He was an undercover man but, unlike most undercover men, everyone knew him and feared him. He was big and strong, liked good wine and luscious women and was always forking over money to flocks of ragged stool-pigeons who tipped him off. He dressed fit to kill and was very well-mannered. And when the spying was over

39

for the day he came back to his sumptuous apartment and slapped Miss Ball around. When he got tired of slapping her around he nuzzled her, and bit her on the neck, and then threw her a gold *lamé* dress and they went out on the town where, in the middle of their expensive dinner, they were set upon by the squat shaven-headed crooks. Her undercover agent boyfriend was a real bastard, but you couldn't help liking the guy. In the end he ran out on Miss Ball. To do good.

"Here he comes now," said Miss Ball to Mr. Gibbon.

Mr. Gibbon turned away and began staring at the loudspeaker of the radio.

"Good morning." It was Herbie.

"You're early," said Miss Ball. "You're an early bird."

"*Shh.*" Mr. Gibbon did not turn. He seemed to be shushing the radio.

"I try," Herbie whispered.

"That's what counts."

"Shut up," said Mr. Gibbon. He still did not turn away from the radio, and the radio happened to be playing the National Anthem. As soon as he said it the anthem ended, and the effect was quite incongruous. *Shut up* and then the end of that glorious song.

"Your first breakfast," said Miss Ball.

"Yes," said Herbie. "My first breakfast."

"Did you ever shoot a machine-gun?" Miss Ball leaned toward Herbie.

"Beg pardon?"

"A machine-gun." She chewed her toast. "Did you ever shoot one?"

"No. Why?" Herbie twitched.

"Just asking, that's all."

"Did *you* ever shoot a machine-gun?"

"No."

"But you'd *like* to shoot one. Is that it?"

"No." Miss Ball laughed. "Really no."

"You're interested in guns? You collect them or . . ."

"Gosh," said Miss Ball, "I didn't mean to start anything. I was just wondering out loud, just making conversation. Idle conversation I guess you'd call it."

"That's what I call it," Mr. Gibbon said, turning full face upon Miss Ball.

Mr. Gibbon's face was a study in hardened stupidity. It had an old hungry look about it.

Mr. Gibbon's lips kept moving, as if he were silently cursing Miss Ball's idle conversation or finishing his egg. This made his nose—which was pointed and hooked—move also. Mr. Gibbon was wearing a khaki tie, a gray shirt—a sort of uniform.

"I'm not talking to *you*," Miss Ball said petulantly.

"I'm talking to you," said Mr. Gibbon. "I went through three wars just so's I could sit here in peace and quiet and listen to my favorite song. And with you blathering I can't hear myself think, let alone listen to my favorite . . ."

"We have a new boarder."

". . . song," Mr. Gibbon finished. He recovered and said to Herbie, "You been in the army?"

"No."

"No what?"

"*What?*"

"I said, no what?"

"No what?" Herbie shook his head. "What what?"

"*You* haven't been in no army," Mr. Gibbon roared.

"I didn't say I had, did I?"

"Didn't have to."

"Why?"

"Why what?"

"Why," Herbie caught on, "*sir?*"

"'S'better. Sounds a hell of a lot better too. Reminds me of a fella we had in basic. A buddy of mine. He caught on. Didn't sir nobody."

"What happened to him?"

"He learned how."

"How did he learn," said Herbie, "sir?"

"They fixed him up real good. Then he learned."

"Fixed him up?" asked Miss Ball, suddenly becoming involved in the conversation.

"Beat the living stuffings out of him."

"That will be just about enough of that," said Miss Ball.

Mr. Gibbon had gone on eating, however, and did not hear. He chewed slowly, his fork upraised, his eyes vacant, but staring in the general direction of Herbie, as if he had just missed a good chance to beat the living stuffings out of Herbie.

"*Well!*" Miss Ball said, folding her hands and grinning into Herbie's face. "You come from Holly Heights?"

"Yes."

"I've never been there myself, but they say it's nice."

"It's very nice. Like a lot of the nice places it's very, very nice."

"You look like a reader."

"I like to read very much."

"I was never a great reader," Mr. Gibbon offered, in order to signal that he was no longer interested in beating up Herbie.

"What does your daddy do?"

Herbie cringed. He had forgotten for a while that he had a daddy—a father, that is. He thought of the man and then said, "My daddy—my father—was in tools."

43

"*Was* in tools?"

"He used to make them. He's dead now, so he doesn't make them anymore."

"There's good money in tools," said Mr. Gibbon. "And there's still a bundle to be made in tools."

"I was never interested in tools myself," said Herbie. "People say I don't take after my father. Maybe they're right. I don't care about tools, although I realize they're important in their own way—just like people are . . ."

"*Hell* of a lot of money to be made in tools. Specially in machine tools."

"It's almost time for school," said Miss Ball, looking at her Snooz-Alarm, which she carried around with her in the house.

"Your old man make machine tools?"

"Nearly time, I said," Miss Ball announced again.

"You don't mind interrupting an intelligent conversation, do you?" Mr. Gibbon was angry at Miss Ball. He had the habit of never saying anyone's name. He glared in the proper direction instead, to identify the person.

Miss Ball faced him. Then she patted Herbie on the arm and said, "Don't you worry about old grumpy here. That's his way of making friends."

"If I feel like grousing, I grouse," said Mr. Gibbon truculently. "I don't care what people think. I been through three wars."

44

"Which three?" Herbie asked.

"*Which three!*" Mr. Gibbon almost choked. "You hear that?" Mr. Gibbon faced Miss Ball. "That's a laugh." He laughed and then turned back to his breakfast and muttered once again, "Which three. For cry-eye."

"I'd like to talk to you some time about war," said Herbie.

"Any time," said Mr. Gibbon. "I'm always prepared."

"He'll talk your ear off," said Miss Ball.

"I don't think it's a good idea, frankly."

"He always does it. It's his way." Miss Ball spoke as if Mr. Gibbon were not at the table. But he was at the table, studying the horror-mask cutout on the back of the cereal box.

"I mean war," said Herbie.

"So does he," said Miss Ball, amused.

Mr. Gibbon grunted.

"But you'll get used to it. We all do. He's not so bad. Just in the mornings he's a little grumpy. Isn't that right, Grumpy?"

"You're going to be late for school."

"Imagine," said Miss Ball. "You both work at the same factory. Isn't that something?"

Herbie admitted that it was something, and then he saw Mr. Gibbon rise, click his heels, and march out the door. Herbie gulped his milk and followed.

5

Herbie trotted, skipped, and hopped after Mr. Gibbon, who was striding grimly down the sidewalk to the Kant-Brake Toy Factory. At first Herbie held the letter in his hand, but when he noticed that the envelope was getting sweaty and wrinkled he stuffed it into his pocket. Herbie had asked Mr. Gibbon who the man was whose name was on the envelope (a certain Mr. D. Soulless). "The old man himself," Mr. Gibbon had answered, without breaking his stride.

At the front gate there was a sentry box, striped with red and white, and in front of it, at attention, was a militarily dressed (V. F. W. blue cap, braids, puttees, combat boots, breeches, assorted stained medals and insignia) though very old sentry. The sentry held a thick M-1 rifle (obs.) in place.

Mr. Gibbon snapped the sentry a salute and started through the gate with Herbie. "He's okay," said Mr. Gibbon to the sentry, jerking his thumb in Herbie's direction. "Gonna see the old man. Business."

But the sentry came forward. Herbie saw that he was about ninety. He levelled his rifle at Herbie. The rifle shook and then inscribed an oval on Herbie's chest.

"Don't you move," the sentry said threateningly.

"He's okay," Mr. Gibbon said. But he did not insist.

"Can't let him through without no authorization from the old man hisself."

"He's new," said Mr. Gibbon, but Mr. Gibbon's heart was not in it. Rules were rules. He knew better than to ask the sentry to do something that was not allowed. He knew the sentry well. Skeeter, the guys called him. He had towed targets during one of the wars.

"I got my orders," said the sentry. His rifle was still weaving at Herbie and once it even stabbed Herbie's shirt.

Herbie tried to shrug, but he was afraid to shrug too hard. He thought it might make the gun go off. He imagined a fist-sized slug bursting through his chest.

"I'll call the C.O.," said Mr. Gibbon. "I'll clear it through him."

"How am I supposed to know who you are? Every man's a Red until he can show me different," the sentry said. Mr. Gibbon walked up the road to the main office. Apparently the sentry saw no point in talking to Herbie. He stopped. Perhaps he was out of breath.

"Lots of security around here," said Herbie, hoping to calm the man down.

"Maybe," was the cryptic reply.

"I mean, for a toy factory. Most toy factories don't have this much security, do they?"

"Do they? I don't know," the sentry said coldly. "I never been in *most* toy factories. Just this one is all."

"Just asking."

"I heard you."

"A toy factory with a guard," Herbie said to himself, and started to shake his head and smile.

"You think it's funny?"

"Yes," said Herbie. "No."

"Pretty funny for a wise guy, aren't you?"

"You think so?" It came out in the wrong tone of voice: an unintentional, but very distinct, rasp.

"I think so."

"I was thinking," said Herbie. "With you standing there with that loaded gun, waving it at people like me and getting mad . . ." Herbie's voice trailed off, then started up again. "I was thinking, someone might get hurt. . . ."

"Like you."

Herbie nodded. "Like me. Exactly."

"I got a job to do."

"That's what I was saying. A toy factory with a guard."

"I'd shoot you down as look at you. I used to tow targets."

"I wouldn't doubt it."

49

"I seen action. Lots of it."

Herbie noticed that although the sentry's body was faced in his direction and the sentry's rifle was still pointed in the general area of Herbie's chest, the sentry's eyes were glazed, his mind was somewhere else. Perhaps on some of the action he had seen.

"Damn right," said the sentry. "Plug you right there, if I had a mind to. I plugged lots of guys before. Wise guys, just like you, mostly. We had more trouble with the wise guys than the Jerries. So we plugged the wise guys. It was war. You can't have wise guys in a war, or smart alecks either. I plugged my best friend. He used to wise around the place all the time. Had to give him the payoff. Sure, I hated to do it—he was my buddy, but that's the way you lose wars. The wise guys lose them for you."

Herbie looked at the rifle riding up and down his torso. It had one eye.

"I got my orders. I wouldn't care. I'd just *shoot!*" The last word flew out angrily with a fine spray of spit.

Herbie backed toward the gate and the safety of the sidewalk. The guard still aimed his rifle where Herbie had been. Just as Herbie was thinking seriously about running back to Miss Ball's house Mr. Gibbon appeared.

"You been cleared," he shouted to Herbie. "It's okay, Skeeter. He's been cleared by the old man."

Skeeter, the sentry, wheeled around and jerked his rifle at the sky. Both Mr. Gibbon and Herbie flattened themselves on the driveway. Herbie waited for the explosion, numbness, death. But there was no explosion.

"I woulda shot," said Skeeter, the sentry.

"I don't blame you," said Mr. Gibbon. He understood security.

Herbie said nothing.

Mr. Gibbon took Herbie to the main office and said, "You're on your own now, sojer."

On the door to the main office was a plaque which read, GEN'L DIGBY SOULLESS, UNITED STATES ARMY (RET'D.).

"Come in!" bellowed a voice from inside.

Herbie nodded to the bellow and went into the office of the retired general. Inside, he said good morning and started to sit down in a large chair.

"Don't bother to sit down," said the man. He was, like Skeeter at the gate, wearing a fancy uniform. Very authentic-looking. "You won't be here long."

Herbie remembered the letter. He pulled it out and handed it across the desk.

The man with the fancy uniform read the letter quickly, then looked up. "So," he said. He fixed his eyes on Herbie, wet his lips, and began to croak affectionately. He had known Herbie's father damn well, about as well as one person can know another one. At least, the man qualified, these days. They had bowled together, had dime-beers together, grabbed ass together and been in tools together. Oh, it was all right in tools with the elder Gneiss, but he—after his retirement from the army—had moved up the ladder and built Kant-Brake from willing men and muscle, real pioneers, men with dreams and a lot of dough. Herbie's father had gotten married and stayed in tools. General Soulless couldn't stand tools himself. That is, tools *as* tools. He wanted to make something useful. He had a dream, too, if that didn't sound like bullshit. He went into war toys.

But he still had a hell of a lot of respect for Herbie's old man. They had done a lot of things together when they were young. He could write a book about all those crazy adventures. He could write twenty books. How they used to go swimming in the raw, fishing in the lake. Times had changed, but he still couldn't forget Herbie's father, a scrappier little guy there never was.

Herbie stood on one leg and then on the other. He agreed that his father certainly was a scrappy little guy. Herbie said that, of course, was before he was his father.

The man laughed. "I'll say!" he croaked. "You scrappy like your dad?"

"I guess so," said Herbie, "yes." But all that Herbie could remember about his scrappy old dad was the large bowling ball with the undersized finger holes.

"Them were the days," the man said. He went on. He could—no he *should*—write a book about those days. It'd be a goddamned funny book, too. He said that some day he would write it. A big fat book. He'd put everything in it that had ever happened to Herbie's scrappy dad and him. All the roughnecks and shitheads, all the skinny girls with flat chests and freckles, and that hungry rougey old bag they met one night. Did Herbie know about that? Probably not. But the retired general wouldn't leave out a single word. He'd get it all down on paper when he had the chance. It wouldn't be any sissy novel either. It would be a big lusty novel, sad sometimes, with all a kid's important memories of growing up. The way kids see things, since kids really knew what was going on. That's why the retired general was in that business, he said. He liked kids.

Herbie wished the man luck with the novel. Then for no reason at all he thought of his mother. There was a novel, or maybe a folk opera: jazzy tunes, honky-tonk, the swish of brushes on drums as his mother gobbles sadly in front of the TV, a blue tube lighting up her bowls of ice cream. And then, mountainous, glutinous, and jiggling with the rhythm of the tunes, she slides out of the house, down the street to the brink of her open grave and then flops ever so quietly into it.

"So you want a job, eh?"

"Yessir."

"Like the place?"

"Very much."

"It's not just any old toy factory, y'understan'," said the man. "We got style—that's what counts nowadays. I mean, saleswise. You can't fool kids. Kids are the darnedest little critics of things. They know when you're putting the screws to them."

"Sure do," said Herbie.

The man continued. Kids were funny. They knew what they wanted, a certain color, size, shape, etc. They got books out of the library and studied about war and crap. They knew what was going on. If the retired general had his way he'd hire young kids, real young, impressionable, scrappy little bastards, instead of old men. But he'd get arrested, wouldn't he?

After saying this, the man laboriously got up out of his chair, walked around the desk to Herbie, and then skidded his fist over Herbie's chin in what was meant as a playful gesture of affection that old men become incapable of and, often, arrested for. The man went back to his chair heavily and repeated that he liked kids a lot.

Herbie said that if it weren't for kids where would they be? Then he thought of what he said and licked his lips.

Just the same, the man agreed.

Herbie said that he was absolutely right.

"You're a lot like your old man." The man wiped his mouth with a chevroned sleeve.

Herbie tried to look as scrappy as possible. He looked at the twenty dollars' worth of ribbons and string on the retired general's chest. He tried to forget that his father was a runt and hoped that the retired general would forget it too.

"You got yourself a job, son."

The man then introduced himself as General Digby Soulless, Retired, and took Herbie down into the workshops. Herbie would be in the motor pool with Mr. Gibbon. Herbie would have to know the ropes. He was issued a uniform, shoes, and a rucksack. He put on the uniform and worked for the rest of the day in silence. The rest of the men were good to him, told him dirty jokes and took him into their confidence. They saw that the old man himself had brought Herbie down and introduced him. So this is the army, Herbie thought throughout the day. At the end of the day Herbie went out through the main gate with the rest of the men. And when Skeeter, the sentry, saw Herbie approaching in uniform, he saluted grandly and nearly dropped his rifle.

6

Work at Kant-Brake went on. Millions of tanks, Jeeps, and rockets rolled off the assembly line without a hitch. Herbie got to enjoy working once he learned the routine. He sent money home, got an occasional note from his mother saying that she was keeping alive and well. Life at Miss Ball's was fairly pleasant. Mr. Gibbon grumbled, barked a lot, but did not bite. Miss Ball was a sympathetic person, although she wore very heavy make-up. Herbie did not expect a woman with a perfectly white face, a little greasy red bow for lips, and hair that was sometimes blue, sometimes as silver as one of Kant-Brake's fuselages, and always tight with hard little curls, to be a nice lady. But she was kind and tolerant. She said she owed all her tolerance to her membership in the D.A.R.

Herbie talked to Miss Ball about many things. She knew the movements of any actor, actress, or starlet he could name: who was queer, who was in Italy, who was really seventy and said he was forty-four. And late one evening, when they were talking about marriages, Herbie asked Miss Ball if she had ever been married. Juan was taken for granted. He was just one of the hired help and didn't count.

"Sure," said Miss Ball, "I've been married."

"No kidding?"

"Wouldn't think so, would you?"

"Why not?"

"Maybe I'm not the type."

"What's *the type*?"

"With a flowered apron, hamburgers sizzling on the griddle, with shiny teeth and bouncy hair. My hair's all dull and streaky."

"That's the *type*?" Herbie thought only of his mother. She hadn't had any of the things Miss Ball mentioned. All she had, as a married woman, was a scrappy little runt of a husband.

"That's what they say."

"I never heard it."

"But," Miss Ball smiled, "did you put your thinking-cap on?"

"Well, what about him?"

"Him? You mean my *hus*band?" A laugh did not quite make it out of Miss Ball's throat, although there were signs of it approaching. It never came.

58

"Yes," said Herbie. "Your husband. The man you married."

"Whatever became of him," sighed Miss Ball. "What shall I say? Shall I say we loved and then were, as they say, estranged? Or shall I tell you he was a big producer who did me dirt? Or shall I tell you he was a poor boy, a very mixed up young man that I found committing highly unnatural acts in the summer house with another twisted little fellow? Shall I tell you he was a bald-faced liar? Yes, that's what he was, a liar."

Miss Ball tried to flutter her hand to her lips. But it was late in the evening and her hand never got beyond her left breast.

". . . he *did* do me wrong. Very, very wrong. But I'm not him, thank God. I am not that man and I don't have to live with his terrible conscience—I'd hate to be in his shoes right now."

"Where is he?"

"He's dead."

"I wouldn't like to be in his shoes either," said Herbie.

"There was a bit of the Irish in him, you know," said Miss Bail, abandoning the dramatic-hysteric role and lapsing into what she intended to be a brogue. "A bit of the oold sahd . . ." She stopped and then went on. "Full o' blarney, he was." Miss Ball just could not get a twinkle out of her heavily made-up eyes. Her eyelids kept sticking. "The sonofabitch."

Venom frothed and boiled out of some hidden nodes in Miss Ball's body, surprising Herbie. Miss Ball cracked all her make-up to flakes in her rage. She was such a nice old lady, Herbie thought. And now Herbie didn't know her.

"The no-good sonofabitch. Want to know what he used to do? Hated me so much he used to get up early in the morning, before me. Then he'd sit down—it was four in the morning—and just eat his Jungle Oats as nice as you please. Then coffee. Had to have his coffee. Then, when he finished, he'd take the coffeemaker, the electric coffeemaker, and pull the screws out and screw the top off and wind the friction-tape off the plug I had to fix about ten times because he was too lazy. Then he'd fill the sink with hot soapy water and dunk the coffeemaker into the water and leave it in the suds."

"And where were you?"

"I was in bed! That's where you belong at four in the morning—not taking coffeepots apart so your wife can't have her coffee. But it doesn't stop there," said Miss Ball. "Not by a long shot it doesn't stop there."

"He does sound like a skunk," Herbie offered.

"He was a regular S.O.B.," said Miss Ball. "And I hope you know what that means."

"I guess . . ."

"But that wasn't all, because then he had to yell in my room at the top of his lungs."

"He *had* to?"

"That was part of the thing, the act he did. He always did the same thing every morning."

"So what did he yell?"

Miss Ball stood up from her wing-chair and cupped her hand to her mouth like an umpire. She even raised her other arm as if she were signaling a safe catch. She twisted her mouth and shouted in an ear-splitting voice, "*When your ole lady died and went straight to hell she should have taken you with her and such and such and so and so!*" Miss Ball recovered, stared wide-eyed and said, "I wouldn't repeat some of the things he said to me those times."

"Then he left."

"Then he left," said Miss Ball. "But he came back."

"Really?" Herbie steadied himself for another blast. He was getting worried.

"He left in the morning. In the night he came back. He went to church and work in between."

"Church. Which church?"

"The stupid Irish church, that's which church. He was what you might call a Catholic. He had to go to church."

"I thought they just had to go on Sunday."

"They don't."

"That's not what I thought."

"Not on Lent they don't."

61

"But Lent is only a month or two in the winter, isn't it?"

"Don't ask me," said Miss Ball. "It was always Lent in our house. Lent and hate."

"Maybe marriages can be based on hate instead of love," Herbie said.

"Ours was. The girls down at the D.A.R. said to stay away from Catholics if you want to stay tolerant. But I wouldn't listen. Sure, he wasn't all bad—he used to pick up stray cats and stuff. The girls said that's a sign of loneliness. He was probably lonely."

"It was his way," said Herbie. He had been waiting for a good chance to say it.

"Maybe that's it. He was good about cats. And I really couldn't divorce him for taking the coffeemaker apart. You don't walk into a court and say, I want a divorce—my husband takes the coffeepot apart before church every morning. It doesn't sound right. It wouldn't even sound right in a movie if Ava Gardner said it. Besides, who else is there? There aren't that many people in the world that you can just start tossing them away left and right just because they have a certain way about them. That's what love is—sticking with the guy even though he has creepy habits. It's learning to love the creepy habits so you can sleep in the same bed without killing the sonofabitch."

"I thought I'd hate this job at Kant-Brake, but now I like it."

Miss Ball turned all her face on Herbie. "Of course you'll like it. It'll be fun. You'll learn to get the hang of it. Sure, you hated it at first, but every dog has his day. That's part of living."

"My mother needs the money. She's getting along, getting old."

"I'm getting along myself," said Miss Ball.

"She's all alone now," said Herbie. "My father's gone. It's the least I can do."

"I could have been in the movies. Don't think I didn't have lots of chances. But I sacrificed and here I am."

"My mother just can't stop eating because my father died. Life goes on. You've got to keep eating no matter what happens."

"My husband. He kept me going, I guess."

"If it wasn't for her I wouldn't be here." Herbie thought for a moment. "Who knows where I'd be? Maybe in the real army."

"He could laugh. You should have heard him laugh," said Miss Ball. "Like a barrel of monkeys."

"My mother laughs all the time. She laughs at everything."

"He taught me how to laugh, the old fool."

"People don't laugh enough these days. It's good medicine," said Herbie. "Isn't it? I mean, if you don't laugh you'll go crazy."

63

"I still haven't forgotten how."

"Neither have I. Neither has my mother."

"You've got to learn to laugh," said Miss Ball. And to prove it she emitted a little bark, learned undoubtedly from the husband who rose so early in the morning. She laughed wildly, yelping, looking around the room, her eyes darting from object to object, her laughter growing with each object. It was not continuous, but a series of yelps, wet boffoes and barks. She showed no signs of tiring.

Herbie joined her, slowly at first. Then it was a duet.

7

"You gotta know which side of the bed your brother's on," Mr. Gibbon shouted to Herbie over the roar of the machines. But Herbie did not hear. No one heard anyone else at Kant-Brake. That did not stop the employees from talking. It encouraged them. There were no disagreements, no arguments, no harsh words, and still everyone talked nearly all the time. None of that impatient waiting until the other person finished to add your two cents' worth. And since most of the employees had been through many campaigns there were millions of little stories to tell. Happily, each man got a chance to tell them. So when Mr. Gibbon offered his homily to Herbie, Herbie answered by saying that his tooth hurt. And then Mr. Gibbon said that he liked spunky women and asked Herbie if his mother was spunky.

At noon sharp the machines were shut off. The scream of voices persisted for a few moments after the machines were silenced, then, when everyone heard his own voice, the sounds quickly hushed, as if the human voice were something to be avoided.

Mr. Gibbon came over to Herbie and pointed to a bench. They sat on the bench and opened their paper lunch-bags (there was a mess hall, but Mr. Gibbon had said that he could never stand mess halls, even though he was once a cook and could make enough cabbage for, let's face it, an army). They took out their sandwiches and hard-boiled eggs and began whispering. Everyone else at Kant-Brake was whispering as well. They always whispered at lunch hour. Mr. Gibbon asked Herbie about his family. They continued their lunch, whispering between bites.

Herbie said his mother was his family.

"No kin?"

"Nope."

"Friends of the family?"

"Couple."

"No brothers?"

"Uh-unh."

"Aunts?"

"No kin. None."

"Girlfriends, though."

"Used to."

"'Smatter now?"

"Nothing."

66

"Get one."

"Got one."

"What's your mother like?"

"Okay. Still alive. Pretty strong woman."

"Spunky?"

"You might say so."

"Your old man's . . . ah . . ."

"Dead."

"Passed away, huh?"

"That's what the man said."

"What man? You pullin' my leg? You shouldn't fool with things like that."

"Things like what?"

"Like saying your old man's dead."

"My old man's dead. Dead and [bite] gone [swallow]."

"Stop that."

"Tell *him* that."

"Wait'll you get my age."

"I'm waiting."

"You'll see."

"Sure."

"It's a crime to talk about your old man like that. You should *never* fool with things like that. They should horsewhip everyone under a certain age once a week."

"Who should?"

"The government should."

"Who's gonna buy the whips? Who's gonna do the whipping?"

"Simple. The police. They should do it in public."

"They should kill old men and old ladies. How'd you like that?"

"Don't like it."

"Now you know how I feel."

"Your poor mother. I feel for her, I really do."

"I'm the one that's supporting her."

"That's the least you can do. The very least."

"She's not so poor. She gets enough to eat."

"So you get enough to eat and you're not poor. You got a lot to learn about people, sonny."

"You got a lot to learn about my mother."

"Mothers got hearts. Hearts got to be fed, too."

"With love. Ha-ha."

"With love."

"I can't swallow that."

"Food isn't enough. You'll learn."

"Don't tell me about my own mother, okay? I like her a lot. Maybe more than your mother."

"You don't even know my mother."

"But you meet her and then decide. She raised me, okay. Never hit me once. Now she goes and makes me get this job. She doesn't have it so bad and certainly isn't poor."

"I'll be the judge of that."

"She likes to eat. She eats like a hog."

"What's wrong with eating?"

"No one said anything's wrong with eating."

"I'm an old man. Ate my way through three wars."

"It's some people's hobby. It's her job."

"I'm partial to eating myself," said Mr. Gibbon after a pause.

And they both went on eating.

After work Mr. Gibbon said, "I'd like to meet your mother. Bet she's a fine woman."

Herbie thought a moment. He had told his mother that he would come home once in a while. The weekend was coming and if Mr. Gibbon came Herbie wouldn't have to explain the Kant-Brake operation to her. Mr. Gibbon would do all the talking. Herbie wouldn't have to say a word.

"I'm going home on Friday. You can come along if you want."

"Well," said Mr. Gibbon, "I'd like that fine. There's not a hell of a lot to do on the weekend you know. Just my paper bags and cleaning my brass and such. And Miss Ball's got that gentleman friend that usually drops in."

Herbie felt foolish. There he was, walking down the street with an old man. But not just any old man. No, this old man was a real fuddy-duddy. There was something queer about it. Mr. Gibbon was taller than Herbie, like a big bear, a bear with a cardboard rump ambling next to a little monkey of a boy. It was Herbie and not Mr. Gibbon that had simian features.

It looked as though there should be a leash between them. One of them should have had a collar on, but it was a toss-up as to which one should be holding the leash.

Herbie had never walked so close to an old man before. Or an old lady, either. That included his mother. Herbie's mother didn't get out much. So when she opened the door to greet them her complexion was the color of newsprint, the kind of skin color that one would expect of a person who lived in a living room, slept on a sofa, and ate chocolates with the shades drawn. To Herbie she looked disturbingly well.

She motioned for them to sit down. The TV show wasn't over yet. She kept her eyes fixed on the blue tube and shook a fistful of chocolates at some chairs. The screen jaggered and the picture went to pieces. Herbie got up to adjust the set. Mrs. Gneiss waved him back to his seat. Then she stomped on the carpet with her foot. Her shapeless felt slipper came off, but her bare foot raised itself for another go. The TV snapped back to life, the picture composed itself on the command of Mrs. Gneiss's big foot.

The show went on for several hours. First there was a newsreel, then something entitled "Irregularity and You," then a half-hour of folk songs which concerned themselves with bombs and deformed babies, then a documentary about the human scalp, a dance show complete with disc jockey showed teenaged girls and boys bumping themselves against each other, and finally a panel of Negroes and Mexicans discussed who had been abused the most seriously. When they started feverishly stripping off their shirts to show their wounds and scars, Mrs. Gneiss stomped on the floor again and the TV shut itself off.

"Television," Mr. Gibbon said. And that was all he said.

Mrs. Gneiss looked at him. She chewed at him.

"Mr. Gibbon," Herbie said, "this is my mother."

"Well, any friend of Herbie's," said Mrs. Gneiss. Then she picked up a large piece of chocolate. It was an odd shape, perhaps in the shape of a fish. She threw it into her mouth, and once her mouth was filled she said, "Can I offer you something to eat?"

Herbie swallowed, determined not to vomit.

"Say," said Mr. Gibbon, "is that an Eskimo Pie?"

"Thipth," said Mrs. Gneiss. But she could not speak. She wagged her finger negatively.

"Looks like one," said Mr. Gibbon. "Years ago we used to have them. My buddies used to eat 'em like candy."

"They *were* candy, weren't they?" said Mrs. Gneiss, once she had swallowed most of the chocolate.

71

"You got something there," said Mr. Gibbon.

"Mr. Gibbon was in three wars," said Herbie.

"What ever happened to Eskimo Pies," said Herbie's mother.

"That's what I say," said Mr. Gibbon brightening.

"Even if they did have them today they'd be little dinky things."

"That's the God's truth," said Mr. Gibbon. "Years ago the Hershey Bars were the big things."

"Nowadays they're a gyp," said Mrs. Gneiss. "I try to tell Herbie how much he's being gypped nowadays, but he never listens. He just laps up all those lies."

"Big ideas!" Mr. Gibbon started. He crept over to the sofa and sat next to Mrs. Gneiss. When he got there he was almost out of breath. "Big ideas," he finally said again. "I think years ago people were smarter than they are now, but they didn't have any smart ideas like people do now."

"Right!" said Herbie's mother. "I knew a lot of people in my day, but I never met one with any smart ideas. Boy, I remember those big Hersheys!"

"Trollies, too," said Mr. Gibbon. "Years ago we used to hitch rides on 'em. Loads of fun, believe me. But today? I'd like to see you try that today?"

"Try *what* today?" asked Herbie.

"Hitchin' a trolley-bus," said Mr. Gibbon.

"You mean riding?"

72

"No, I mean *hitching*. You crawl on the back of the thing and hold on with your fingernails. Doesn't cost a penny. Nowadays you'd get killed on a bus. You could do it easy then."

"What for?" Herbie asked. But no one answered.

Herbie's mother and Mr. Gibbon continued to talk excitedly of the past. They talked of penny candy, nickel ice creams and dime novels. Mr. Gibbon said that he had once bought a whole box of stale White Owl cigars for five cents and then smoked the whole boxfull under his front steps. He had been violently ill.

"The things you could do with a nickel," Herbie's mother said nostalgically.

"Remember Hoot Gibson?"

"Whatever became of Hoot Gibson?"

"The old story."

"Isn't it always the way."

"No one cares."

They talked next of Marx and Lincoln. Not the famous German economist and the Great Emancipator, but Groucho and Elmo. Mr. Gibbon went on to tell how he had run away from school at a very early age. He said that kids nowadays didn't have the guts to do that. How he used to go fishing with a bent pin and a bamboo pole, how he had joined the army at a very early age. No fancy ideas. Nowadays it was the fancy ideas that were ruining people.

"I don't have any fancy ideas," said Herbie.

"You *do*, and you know it," said his mother, silencing him.

"Years ago," said Mr. Gibbon, "good food, clean living, nice kids."

"Nowadays," said Mrs. Gneiss, "I don't know how I stand it."

Mr. Gibbon said that he had known a girl in his youth that looked just the way Herbie's mother must have looked. Full of freckles and vanilla ice cream, plump, but not fat. Just the prettiest little thing on earth!

"You'll stay, of course," said Mrs. Gneiss.

"Course," said Mr. Gibbon. "Us old folks got a lot of things to talk about."

"Sure do," said Mrs. Gneiss.

"Probably wouldn't interest the youngster," said Mr. Gibbon. "Now if I'm imposing you just tell me to scoot the blazes out of here."

"*Imposing!* I should say not. We'll just pop a couple of TV dinners in the oven. No trouble *ay-tall*! Unless you mind instant coffee."

"Drink it all the time. Makes me big and strong," said Mr. Gibbon, his eyes glinting, his lips wet and pink.

"You're a card," said Mrs. Gneiss.

"Not so bad yourself, Grandma!"

"Ha-ha-ha," said Mrs. Gneiss.

74

"So's your ole man," said Mr. Gibbon.

"I'm tired," said Herbie. "I think I'll go to bed." He took ten dollars out of his pay envelope and gave his mother the remainder. She thanked him. Herbie stared at the money on his mother's lap. Then he went to bed.

Just before he got into bed he heard Mr. Gibbon say, "They had all-day suckers then. You never see an all-day sucker nowadays. Not one."

Throughout the night Herbie was awakened by wheezing and groaning and the creaking of springs. That was that. He tried to prevent his mind from making a picture of it, but the more he tried the sharper the picture became. He switched on the radio to keep his mind off the noise in the next room. The news was on. The president had just had his kidney stone and gallbladder removed. The commentator said, "the stone had the appearance of an irregular gold nugget or arrowhead. The opened gallbladder was reddish brown and the greenish half-inch gallstone, which infected, was visible in the lower left fold near the cystic duct. . . ." After this the president himself came on and said that he just had to get out of the hospital and do his work, even if it meant further infection. There was a war on and that had to be tended to.

With the radio buzzing about the movements of troops, Herbie went softly to sleep.

8

Mr. Gibbon became a frequent visitor to Herbie's house.

Herbie stopped going home altogether. Instead, he went for walks around Mount Holly, met a girl and took her to bed. The first time they went to bed the girl said, "New, new, new!" which struck Herbie as odd. But they made love just the same. Afterward, when Herbie offered the girl a cigarette, she said simply, "New, thank you." Like Herbie the girl had no plans, and Herbie had no plans for her.

Herbie's mother became more hostile, but also less demanding. Herbie sent her less and less money each week. She did not mention this in her letters. Instead she sent more letters and started using phrases like, "Life is just beginning for me," "a big new world is opening up," "Charlie has taught me how to live and love," "old people have feelings too," "the sky's the limit" and "dawn is breaking." They were very uncharacteristic phrases. Mr. Gibbon had apparently kindled a flame inside his mother, Herbie thought.

Indeed, Mr. Gibbon had done just that. Mrs. Gneiss, Mr. Gibbon, and Miss Ball had started an outing club to get fresh air. They walked, brought cold lunches, ate devilled eggs, and listened to their transistor radio. Some color—not much, but *some*—came into Mrs. Gneiss's face. It would be rash to say she had a ruddy complexion, but it certainly wasn't chalky. It was lemony after a few picnics, and then it took on a slightly veined pinkish hue. The outings were doing her good. The walking increased her appetite, which Mr. Gibbon was now paying for. She gained weight, but the new bulk was not perceptible. Only other really fat people notice changes in a fat person. Mrs. Gneiss was not embarrassed by the added weight. She repeated that everything she ate turned to fat. There was no question that she was coming alive. She had started wearing dresses and muumuus and had burned her tattered kimono. She took to walking and sweating. Firmness came into her hams and trotters just as color came into her jowls.

One Sunday the outing was held at the Mount Holly Botanical Gardens. Mr. Gibbon, as usual with map and compass, had led the way. They spread their blanket under a tree and ate, then turned on the radio and listened to news of the president's kidneys and gallstones and negotiations with what Mr. Gibbon called "The Yellow Peril," and then lolled about on the grass. The sky was filled with clouds that kept getting in the way of the sun. This irritated Mr.

Gibbon. He said so. "Those clouds aggravate me," was what he said. Lots of things galled him, he said, but life was still worth living. He said that he owed a great deal to Mrs. Gneiss. He had thought that his life was over, but Mrs. Gneiss had convinced him that he could move on. "If an old battle axe like me and an old biddy like you can fall in love," he said, "then anything is possible." He had wondered about this before. Now he knew it for sure.

"Charlie," said Mrs. Gneiss, "you're the sweetest man in the world." Without pausing she added, "Pass the salad, Miss Ball."

"Just because you're a certain age," said Miss Ball, passing the salad to Mrs. Gneiss, "doesn't mean there's anything you can't do. Why, it should be easier when you're old because you know more, but no one tries. That's the fly in the ointment really."

"Sure is," said Mr. Gibbon. "Sure is. Why, look at us. Three folks with lots of spunk left."

"Oodles of spunk left," Miss Ball interjected. "Oodles."

"And it's all going to waste. We're just wasting away," said Mrs. Gneiss, her mouth dripping mayonnaise.

Mr. Gibbon smacked his lips in disgust. "That green-horn doctor had the nerve to boot me out of the army. Why, I was old enough to be his father! If I had stayed in they wouldn't be having so much trouble with their wars. Send me in! Give me fifteen men of my own choosing and we'll blast all those yellow bastards to kingdom come! I been in three wars and I won all three. Give me another one, that's what *I* say!"

"Oh Charlie, you're a real campaigner," said the delighted Mrs. Gneiss.

"Why not victory?" said Mr. Gibbon. "Just send me over!"

Miss Ball had been shaking her head. "I'm a Daughter of the American Revolution," she said, "and I've seen a lot of our boys murdered in cold blood by the Communists. The real problem is right here in our midst: the You-Know-Whos. If we didn't have so many of them—and they're all as Red as they are black, as I'm sure you know—this country would be ours again and we could put a big fence around it. We could start life all over again in our own backyard. You don't have to scurry all over the world with your planes and such to find the enemy. Not when he's there, smack in Mount Holly, emptying your trash-can, shining your shoes, cleaning your car, grinning at you, lying in his teeth, taking food out of your mouth and money out of your pocket!"

"That's it in a nut-cake!" said Mr. Gibbon, jumping to his feet. "The problem is right here. We can't ignore it. And I say the best fertilizer for a piece of land is the footprints of its owner!"

Saying this Mr. Gibbon looked across the grass, past the bunches of flowers, through the trees to the clouds—those fickle things that kept getting themselves in the way of the sun. He frowned at the clouds as if the clouds represented everything foul, all the You-Know-Whos that kept trying to prevent decent folk from having sunny days.

"So we sit here blabbing about it," said Mrs. Gneiss. "Why don't we *do* something about it?"

"What can we do?" asked Mr. Gibbon. "Oh, I know. It's coming all right. Hate and bitterness."

"I hate bitterness," said Miss Ball.

"It wouldn't be so bad," said Mr. Gibbon, "if they were just shining your shoes and emptying your trash-cans. That wouldn't be so bad. But did you ever see the beat of it when every You-Know-Who in the damn country decides to get uppity? You looked at any movies lately? They're up there doing a soft-shoe with our womenfolk. Been in any drug stores the last year or two? There they are, sucking up Cokes. Been in a bank lately ["A *bank!*" Mrs. Gneiss gasped]—like that bank in town maybe? There they are, putting their crumby fingers over all the money. I tell you, it makes my blood boil! Why, I was in that bank cashing my pension check just the other day. Stood in line. There's one behind the counter. Went to another counter. *Another* one in front of me and one in back. Complain, I says to myself. Do something. Decided to have a word in private with the manager. Waited in line outside his office. Finally went in. You guessed it! A coon in the chair! What could I do? I still haven't cashed the damn pension check."

"It's too much," said Miss Ball.

"Something should be done about it," said Mr. Gibbon.

Miss Ball tapped Mr. Gibbon on the shoulder, narrowed her eyes and said, "Sonny, you can do anything you want if you just get the bee in your bonnet."

They returned to Mount Holly to find Herbie slumped dejectedly in Miss Ball's wing-chair. He was surprised to see his mother. He couldn't remember having seen her out of the house for years. But he soon recaptured his dejection. There was a slip of yellow paper in his hand. A draft notice. Herbie was to report for his physical the next day. The country was at war.

Part Two

9

They finally settled on a bank robbery. "It's the logical thing to do when you stop and consider that I can't even cash my U.S. Army pension check, the place is so loaded with coons and commies," Mr. Gibbon explained. It would take some planning, but they would be able to do it. The robbery of a communist bank would prove to the world that old folks still had a lot of spunk left.

The robbery became all the more important after Herbie passed his army physical. He was due to leave for boot camp in four days.

"You're a very lucky man," Mr. Gibbon said to Herbie.

Herbie thought otherwise. He didn't want to go. But he didn't know why he didn't want to go. At first he thought of Kant-Brake. The place was full of soldiers. They weren't bad. But there was something missing, and when Herbie finally thought of what was missing, a chill shot through the holes in his bones. Death was missing from Kant-Brake. That's what the army made him think of: death.

"This is a time for courage. This is a time when men of all races and creeds must join hands and make the world a safe place. This is not a time for us to waver. This is not a time for us to lose our nerve. This is a time for us to be strong," the president had said in his now-legendary "This Is a Time" speech to Congress. Charlie Gibbon had wept.

For Herbie this was not a time to go into the army. Be strong? He had seen all those people carrying signs.; the boys with the bushy hair and the woollen shirts; the girls with no make-up and necklaces made out of macaroni. They didn't want war. Herbie had seen them dragged, kicking and screaming, into police vans. They didn't think that this was a time to be strong. But when they mentioned God, Herbie thought of nothing. He just didn't want to go. He had no reason for refusing. He would have felt foolish with a sign. A beard would have made his face pimply.

And then, the day before he was to go to boot camp, he thought of his reason for not wanting to go into the army. I'm afraid, he thought: I don't want to die, I don't want to throw bombs at people and shoot guns, I don't want to sleep in the jungle, march around in the mud and get shot at. Herbie remembered how quickly the sweet old Miss Ball had turned into an angry, cursing old bag. There was Mr. Gibbon's buddy that didn't say "sir" and got the living stuffings beaten out of him. There was Skeeter's pal, the wise guy, that had to be shot because wise guys lose wars for you.

Dying is easy, Herbie thought. So I go and get killed. My mother watches television. Mr. Gibbon crawls all over her, folds his paper bags in peace. Miss Ball and Juan have their jollies without the secret police breaking down the door. I die and life goes on in Mount Holly.

Herbie didn't hate anyone. He had even stopped wishing for his mother's death. Mr. Gibbon was in charge now. The care and feeding of Herbie's mother was in Mr. Gibbon's hands. Herbie could stay at Kant-Brake a while longer and make a few extra dollars. But the thought of going into the army scared him limp. Still, he knew that he would be laughed at if he said that his reason for not wanting to go in was strictly that he was chicken-livered. Not even the bushy people that carried the signs on the sidewalk would listen to him. The soldiers certainly wouldn't listen. Herbie pictured himself going up to a general and saying, "I can't fight, sir. I'm scared." The picture faded. A boy with a sign and hair curling all over his horn-rimmed glasses like weeds appeared. Herbie said to the boy, "I don't want to go into the army either. I'm scared." Laughter from the general behind the desk and the boy on the sidewalk spattered Herbie. If you were scared you were no good.

87

So he did not say he was scared. He told no one. He merely sat around the house thinking, my death will keep that television going. If I don't die and someone else dies I'll come back and watch it. At least I have a home to come back to.

The Kant-Brake employees gave Herbie a knife ("Get a few for us, Herbie") and a Kant-Brake Front Lines First Aid Kit, every detail done in perfect scale. A memento. General Digby Soulless slapped Herbie on the back and said that he had gone into the army when he was half Herbie's age. He added, "This is the real thing, boy. Get the lead out of your pants."

On the day Herbie left for boot camp Mr. Gibbon told him how much he envied him. Beans tasted so good cooked in a foxhole. He told him how to creep under barbed wire and bursting guns, how to clean his mess kit while on bivouac (with sand), how to cure rot and so forth. He presented Herbie with a new comb and told Herbie about his aunt. He told Herbie, in a whisper, not to worry about his mom. Mr. Gibbon would take care of her. "Confidentially, she's fat and sassy, and that's just the way I like 'em."

Miss Ball said it thrilled her to know that Herbie was actually going to war. She had read about so many of "our boys" going off, never to be heard from again. Now she could say that she knew one.

Everyone was happy for Herbie and wished him well. His mother was on the verge of tears. She stayed on the verge. She told Herbie very calmly to be a good boy and mind his manners when he got to the war.

Herbie, numb with fear, promised he would. He noticed at the railroad station that their cab held four suitcases instead of two.

"Half the luggage is mine," Mrs. Gneiss said.

"Are you coming along?"

"Goodness, no!" said Mrs. Gneiss. "I'm moving into your room at Miss Ball's. I can be near Charlie that way. I just sold the house."

Herbie nodded goodbye, had his picture taken with the rest of the Mount Holly draftees and the chairman of the Mount Holly draft board, and then joined the mob of boys in the car reserved for them. Herbie sat next to the window and looked at the three old people on the platform waving their hankies.

"Smile, Herbie," his mother said.

"He looks scared to death," Mr. Gibbon said.

"It takes all kinds," Miss Ball said.

10

A dusty twenty-five-watt bulb flickered in Miss Ball's dining-room. The less light the better, they had all decided. The three of them sat around the large mahogany table. Mr. Gibbon was wearing his khakis. His pistol was strapped on. In the dim light of the room the faces of the three people looked even older than they were, bloodless, almost ghoul-ish. Mr. Gibbon was doing all the talking. Only a few of his fifteen teeth were visible and his mouth seemed latched like a dummy's. His whole chin gabbled up and down.

"It's all relative," he was saying. "Even though it doesn't look on the up and up if you say, we gotta rob a bank and we may have to shoot somebody to do it right, it's okay in this case. The country is at stake, and we're the only ones that realize it. Herbie's gone now to do his bit. It's up to us to do our bit even if the only place we can do it is right here in Mount Holly. It's the enemy within we're after. The ones right here grinning at us in our own backyard, as Miss Ball rightly said. It's all relative. Why, I know what it's like to be an American. You take your average American. He can't find his ass with both hands, can he? Bet your life he can't. It's all relative. A commie bank is right here in our midst picking our pockets. And what do we do? We rob that bank right down to the last cent, and if we get any lip from the You-Know-Whos we blast 'em."

Mrs. Gneiss interrupted. "I hate to mention this," she said, "but won't it be against the law to do this? I agree with you one hundred percent that something's got to be done—why, if the communists ran this country we'd starve in two days. But there's the law to think about . . ."

"Let me remind you, Toots, that the law you're so worried about is the law that's made *by* the You-Know-Whos *for* the You Know-Whos. It's not made for decent people like us. The law is made by coons. You got any objections against breaking the coon law? You don't think decent folk should break the coon law? When we rob this bank we'll be heroes. People will be brought to their senses. We'll be doing our country a turn and making the world safe for good government, small government. Now anybody knows that it's not legal to rob a bank. But is it legal for some bastard with dark skin and a party card, all niggered-up with fancy clothes, to walk into *your own bank* and put his fingers all over your money? If that's legal, then what do you call it when decent people want to set an example for their country? Okay, call it illegal if you want. It's all relative. But I'll tell you something: it broke my heart to fight the Germans. I was in that war and, Goddamit, I couldn't help but think that they knew what they were doing all along. I knew it in my heart. I said to myself, Charlie, it's all relative . . ."

"I'm not being an old sceptic," said Miss Ball, "but when we get the money, what do we do with it? I mean, it won't be ours, now will it?"

Mr. Gibbon shook his head in impatience. He had the feeling he wasn't being understood. "We're not going to *steal* the damn money. We're just going to *transfer* it. I suppose we could give it to our favorite charities. Personally, I'd like to see a company like Kant-Brake, a company that's got a heart and thinks about the country, get a little of the dough. I'd like to see the V.F.W. get a little, the Boy Scouts a little, the White Citizens Council a little—spread it around, you see? Lots of people are entitled to it. We'll be fair . . ."

"I'd like to see the D. A.R. get a little bit. They deserve it. They're dedicated."

Mrs. Gneiss did not name her favorite charity. She had some reservations about the robbery. It sounded like a lot of work. Give the You-Know-Whos a few swift kicks. They'd learn. Why rob a bank? And, if they went through with it, it seemed only fair that they themselves should be entitled to some of the cash. She thought of truckloads of

93

Hershey bars, gallons of vanilla ice cream, a new television and, in general, goodies in return for their pains. But she kept silent.

"So it's settled. We knock off the bank and in the process we might have to break a few eggs—that's how you make omelettes, eh? I've got my old trusty .45."

"You mean you might shoot your gun?" Miss Ball asked, her eyebrows popping up.

"Right," said Mr. Gibbon. "How do you like *them* apples?"

Information was needed. Plans had to be made. The next two months were spent poring over detective novels and thrillers, watching spy movies, preparing disguises, masks, and learning to pick up items without leaving fingerprints. Miss Ball was in charge of disguises, Mr. Gibbon had the novels, Mrs. Gneiss had television robbery-movies. Mrs. Gneiss watched all the programs on TV just the same, so it was no extra trouble. It just meant changing channels once in a while. When a detective story was over on one channel, another was starting on another channel. She flicked the knob and settled back with her food.

Mr. Gibbon continued working at Kant-Brake. He was excited about the robbery—it compared favorably with his best experiences in the army. He read the pulp thrillers during the lunch hour and earned the title of "professor" for doing so. The other employees credited the reading and contentment to "Charlie's new lady-friend."

At the end of two months they met again, and this time used the stump of a candle for light. They had a map of Mount Holly in front of them. The Mount Holly Trust Company was marked with an X, and an escape route plotted out on it with one of Miss Ball's E-Z Mark crayons, which she had cleverly snatched from the kindergarten.

Plans were going well, said Mr. Gibbon. They had picked the masks they were going to use, the gloves and special shoes. And they had the escape route decided in advance. There was only one problem. They didn't know where the safe was. They had no floor plan of the bank.

"Oh, shucks!" said Miss Ball. "How can we rob a bank if we don't know where the money is?"

"But the employees know," said Mr. Gibbon.

"A lot of good *that* does us," Mrs. Gneiss said.

"Now just keep your shirts on," said Mr. Gibbon. He explained his plan. What they would do was kidnap one of the bank guards, a white one, and beat the stuffings out of him unless he told them where the safe was. First, of course, they would divulge their plan. But if he didn't want to cooperate they would have to beat him up. He would be able to tell them where the safe was, the strongboxes, the money, the keys, the emergency alarms. "We'll have to kidnap him. It's the only way."

"It's for the good of the country," said Mrs. Gneiss.

Mr. Gibbon said that it wouldn't be too much trouble to get one of the guards. They could lure him to Miss Ball's house. The only thing they needed was a decoy. They had to find a decoy . . .

Her face chalky with make-up, her cheeks rouged with circles, her lips gleaming with the scarlet goo of nearly one whole tube of lipstick, her hair a stiff mass of tight curls, her round body solid with corsets and fixtures, Miss Ball waddled to the back door of the Mount Holly Trust Company and looked for a bank guard to lure.

It was the middle of the afternoon and the sun was very hot. This caused the make-up to run a bit and get very sticky. Beads of perspiration appeared at Miss Ball's hairline, behind her ears and on her neck.

There seemed to be no one to lure. She could see people walking back and forth inside the bank, accountants and tellers. They had little or nothing to do with the storing of money. They just collected it. But no one came out of the back door.

Miss Ball rather enjoyed standing there. Like a siren, she could lure anyone. It gave her a feeling of power. She knew the attraction that a woman's flesh had for men. They couldn't resist it. How many times had Juan, on the pretext of checking the cans of floor wax, covered her with rancid kisses in the broom closet? He couldn't stand it any longer. She understood the urge and let him paw her and grunt. Duty meant nothing. History was full of the stories of men who had given in to the low murmur of beckoning flesh. Fortunes, whole countries had been lost, careers ruined for a few minutes of pleasure in the bed of a beautiful woman.

And then she thought, when you're a decoy you've got to have something to decoy. There was nothing in the back of the Mount Holly Trust Company to lure. A dog sniffed at the hem of her dress and scuttered away, two little boys meandered by throwing spitballs at each other, and once someone peered from the second story of the bank. Miss Ball had glanced up, but before she regained presence of mind enough to wink at the person (one never knew what floor plan he had in *his* pocket) he turned away.

A full hour passed. Miss Ball was tired; her getup was a wreck. Her handbag felt like a large stone. She knew she didn't look as crisp as she had when she arrived. A man likes freshness and vitality in a woman. If much more time passed Miss Ball knew that she would be able to offer none of these.

Then a man appeared at the back door. Miss Ball pressed her lips together. She trembled. The man was white, wearing a blue suit with a matching cap, rimless glasses and a badge. He looked like a bus conductor. But he was a bank guard, and he certainly had a dozen more rolls in the hay left in him. He shuffled out the door with a shopping bag, then went inside and got another bundle and put that beside the shopping bag. After one more trip inside he deposited an umbrella and a pair of rubbers beside the other bundles.

Miss Ball took one step toward the man. She eyed him, fluttered her eyelashes, and said hoarsely, "That's an awful lot of gear for a little man."

"Par' me?" said the man. He squinted through his glasses and coughed. Miss Ball corrected her false impression: the man did not have a dozen rolls in the hay left in him. He had one perhaps, at the most two. Also he was down at the heel and out at the elbow. But it made no difference. He knew the bank inside out. He had the information they wanted.

"Give you a hand?"

The man took another look at Miss Ball. The look cost the man a great effort. He shrugged.

Miss Ball smiled, took the shopping bag and umbrella and led the way. The man picked up the other bundles and the rubbers and followed. *Success*, thought Miss Ball.

They walked along Mount Holly Boulevard and attracted considerable attention.

The man glanced at her once or twice, then cleared his throat and asked her if she minded carrying the bag.

Miss Ball said that she didn't mind doing anything. She winked again.

The man said that he lived across town. Miss Ball said she knew a shortcut. She walked along as briskly as her little legs would move her and finally got to her house. With a sigh she dropped the bags and said that she could go no further.

"That's okay," said the man. "I'll carry the stuff. I was planning to anyways."

Then Miss Ball shrieked. The man dropped what he was carrying.

"For golly sake!" she said. "Look where we are!"

The man said he didn't recognize the place.

"It's my house! Well, isn't that the limit! God help us—it's a miracle."

The man said that he had to be going. He had the week's shopping in the bags, not to mention his wife's umbrella (he called it a bumbershoot).

"You just take your brolly and your shopping and come in. We'll have a little tea. I'm weak. I don't think I can make it into the house."

The man tried to carry Miss Ball into the house. He struggled and panted. Miss Ball remarked that he must have been a very strong man in his youth. The man said he was.

Miss Ball poured a large tumbler full of whisky and handed it to the man. The man drank it and wiped his mouth with his sleeve. "Red-eye," he said.

"Oo! You like your tea, don't you now?"

The man said he didn't mind a spot now and then. He put his arm around Miss Ball and began pinching her breast.

"Not here, darling," said Miss Ball. She tossed her head in the direction of upstairs. Then she stood up and took his hand and pulled him upstairs.

Mr. Gibbon and Mrs. Gneiss tiptoed out of the kitchen and upstairs after them. They listened, their ears against the door.

Inside the room bodies fell, groans resounded, flesh met flesh with slaps and shrieks. Miss Ball squealed, the man roared. Furniture fell and glass broke.

"Lotta spunk left in *her*!" Mr. Gibbon whispered.

"They're having *fun*!" Mrs. Gneiss said. She squeezed Mr. Gibbon's knee.

"Clever little woman," Mr. Gibbon said. "See, she must have learned that in one of the books. She'll get him naked and helpless and then turn on the heat. She'll get him talking about the bank and find out. The man goes away happy and doesn't suspect a thing. Nice as you please."

But there was no talking. The noise had ceased, and now Miss Ball could be heard crying softly. Mr. Gibbon wanted to go right in, but he waited five minutes, and when nothing had changed (the only sound was Miss Ball sniffing) he drew out his pistol and broke the door down.

The room was covered with blood. Sheets and curtains were torn and hanging in shreds, the mirror was shattered, and on the floor lay the bank guard, a large knife-handle sticking out of his back. Bloody handprints were smeared all over the walls and floor. In the corner, a murderous look in his eye, was Juan. His shirt was torn and bloody, his hair bristled. He glowered.

"Dobble cross me! Dat agli gringo bestid don't know what heet heem. I been seeting that share for two jowers."

"Warren!" screamed Miss Ball. He turned. Mr. Gibbon took aim and fired. The impact sent Juan into the wall like a swatted fly. Then he fell, his head making a loud bump on the floor.

"There's two commies out of the way," said Mr. Gibbon. "Get a mop! See if anyone heard! Lock the front door! This is it, boys! It's war! We won a battle but we haven't won the war yet! Fall to, get this mess cleaned up, load the guns!"

Neither Miss Ball nor Mrs. Gneiss moved a muscle. They looked at Mr. Gibbon with horror.

"Hurry up!" said Mr. Gibbon. "You all *deef*?"

11

Mrs. Gneiss's empty suitcases came in handy for storing the dismembered bodies of Juan and the bank guard. At first, Mrs. Gneiss was all in favor of getting the bank guard's fingerprints on the gun and calling the police. They would tell the police that there had been a terrible fight between the two men. Juan had stabbed the guard and then the guard had shot Juan for stabbing him. Tit for tat, so to speak. It made some sense. But Mr. Gibbon saw that if the guard had been stabbed he wouldn't have been able to shoot Juan. Or if Juan were shot the guard would have survived. The murder was without precedent if it was to be believed. They gloomily hacked up the bodies with Mr. Gibbon's hunting knife, stuffed them into Mrs. Gneiss's suitcases and put the suitcases and the clothes into the attic. Miss Ball's Stay-Kleen and Surfy Suds took care of the gore on the rug.

Good Old Providence had done them a turn. The neighbors had miraculously not heard "The Fracas," as

Miss Ball called the double murder. The three comrades had stayed up all night keeping a vigil over the bodies in case the police should come. Then they would have said, yes, we killed the lousy commies. But the police never came. And just as well, the two ladies thought. Mr. Gibbon thought differently: he was convinced that Juan and the bank guard were "in cahoots" (the bank guard more than anyone was a stoolie and a cheat, working for coons as he did). Mr. Gibbon was, as he put it, "pleased as punch" to have plugged Juan, a man he suspected to have been spying on him for nearly a year.

But they had to make short-range plans. The morning after the fracas the three sat around the table (the news was on, but spoke only of the gallstones and the war, both with fervor; the disappearance of a certain bank guard was not mentioned). They looked haggard and mussed, having stayed up all night keeping their vigil. They tried to think of a way to cover up the murder for the time being. They knew that afterward, when the truth about the Mount Holly Trust Company was known (a Communist Front Organization filled with black pinkoes), the murder would be laughed off and their fortune would be secure. Meanwhile, they would have to think of a way to pacify the bank guard's wife. Unless he had been lying when he told Miss Ball that he had to take the groceries home to his wife; maybe he didn't have a wife at all. But how could they find out?

It was Miss Ball that came up with the solution. Without a word she darted upstairs to the suitcases. She came back almost immediately, seated herself as before and dropped a blood-stained wallet on the table. Gingerly—because the plastic wallet was still sticky with the gentleman's blood—Miss Ball picked through it. Out tumbled membership cards, wedding pictures, snapshots of little kids with beach pails, and finally the prize: a picture of the man himself and a woman—obviously his wife; she looked grim and stood apart from him—who was leaning on the very same umbrella that was now resting against the wall upstairs in Miss Ball's attic. On the back of the photograph was printed: "Benny's Fotoshop—Close to You in the Lobby of the Barracuda Beach Hotel," and under that in ballpoint: "Baracuta Beach, 1962." There was also an identification card which read:

Harold Potts, Jr.
1217 Palm Drive
Mount Holly
In case of accident please notify a priest and
Mrs. Ethel Potts
(address as above)

Harold's blood type, a little ragged card with a picture of Jesus on the front and a prayer on the back, and a relic of a tiny piece of cloth that had "touched a piece of the True Cross" sealed in plastic, were also among the valuables. Mr. Gibbon searched in vain for a party card. He came up with a few suspicious-looking documents, but remarked, "He'd be a fool if he carried the thing around with him."

Miss Ball paid no attention to Mr. Gibbon's investigation. She had found what she wanted.

Dear Ethel (Miss Ball wrote),

I wonder if you remember me? We spent those lovely days together at the Barracuda Beach Hotel back in '62. We met briefly during a bridge game. (I can't remember if we were playing, watching, or just passing by the bridge tables—goodness how the memory starts playing tricks as the years go by!)

To make a long story short I met dear old Harold just yesterday at the Mount Holly Trust Company—well, I tell you Harold just couldn't stop talking! We came to my house for tea and just talked and talked and talked of the wonderful days we spent at the Barracuda Beach Hotel back in '62. Harold said he had a touch of gastritis and wanted to go straight to bed, couldn't walk so he said. Well, here it is 10 in the AM and he's still sleeping like a baby! I called the bank and told them he wouldn't be in this morning. I think his tummy needs a rest, frankly Ethel, and I just hate the thought of waking him up, so peaceful he looks. I think he should be improving in the next few days and I'll be sure to have him call you when he wakes up.

I just wanted to let you know that he's safe in the hands of an old friend and that there's no need to get all flustered and call the Missing Persons Bureau! Ha-ha! And that I look forward to more happy days like the ones we spent at the Barracuda Beach Hotel back in '62.

Your old friend,
Nettie

"Perfect," was all Mr. Gibbon said.

"I feel as if I know her," Miss Ball said.

The letter was sent special delivery ("What's thirty cents," Mrs. Gneiss said), without a return address, in a plain envelope. Mr. Gibbon estimated that it would be in Ethel Potts's hands before noon.

"What about Warren's nearest of kin," Mrs. Gneiss asked.

"His nearest of kin? Well, that's *me*, I guess, and *I* know where he is!" Miss Ball said. She did not say it with regret; but there was no joy in her voice either. Miss Ball did not quite know what to think about Juan's death. He had been very pleasant—if a bit jumpy—at first. Only lately had he been asking for more pin-money. He had also recently demanded to move in with Miss Ball, but she had discouraged that. He had a good heart. He had bought things for Miss Ball. He was constantly surprising her with little mementos like the framed picture of Clark Gable or the doilies—he adored doilies for a reason Miss Ball could not even guess at. He had "been with" Miss Ball for about ten months and had never once shown the sort of jealous rage that had prompted him to stab Harold Potts to death.

Juan would have died violently sooner or later. It's in the blood. Better he died in the privacy of Miss Ball's own home than in the gutter. And then maybe Mr. Gibbon was right: maybe Juan *was* a communist. He was certainly dark, a Puerto Rican, there was no denying that! Mr. Gibbon was more familiar with the You-Know-Whos than Miss Ball. She knew that. He knew what he was doing. So goodbye, Juan, *hasta luego* and sleep well, Miss Ball thought.

Meanwhile, Mr. Gibbon was getting impatient. "An itchy trigger-finger," he said. Sooner or later Ethel Potts would start wondering who in Sam Hill was Nettie and might turn the letter over to the police. This would ruin Mr. Gibbon's timing. Floor plan or no floor plan, they would have to rob the bank quickly—at least in the next week or so. Here Herbie was out of boot camp, on his way to the front lines—probably he had nailed a few dozen commies already. A greenhorn! And here was Mr. Gibbon with only these two rather unimportant fellow travellers to his credit.

Mrs. Gneiss agreed. She said she was getting edgy. She didn't enjoy getting edgy. If the robbery was to be done, it should be done as speedily as possible, so that they could all relax and enjoy the rewards and fame the robbery would bring them. She for one didn't want Ethel Potts going haywire and accusing them of killing her husband. But as usual she said nothing more. Charlie knew best. She would wait until he gave the word. The whole thing was his idea, he was the brains and should make the decisions.

"I'd just like to have a look around the bank tomorrow before we go ahead with it," Mr. Gibbon said. Miss Ball should not come along. They didn't want to arouse any suspicions. He and Mrs. Gneiss would just sort of mosey around the bank, seeing what they could see and getting the general layout of the place and, in short, "casing the joint."

Miss Ball said that suited her fine. They sat around the house reading and puttering around for the rest of the afternoon. Mr. Gibbon attended to his long-neglected paper bags; Mrs. Gneiss watched TV. But Miss Ball sat and scowled. Her brow grew more and more furrowed as the afternoon wore on. By five o'clock she was genuinely distressed. Something had just occurred to her. No one took any notice of her, not even when she scribbled a little reminder on the notepad, which she always carried in her apron.

12

Miss Ball kept looking into store windows. Before each one she paused, touched at her hair, pressed her lips together and, reasonably satisfied with the reflection that stared out at her from the foundation garments or baked goods, she walked on toward the doctor's office.

She had begun to worry. She had read of a man who woke up one morning with the beginnings of a sixth finger; she had heard of a lung ballooning to twice its normal size when it had to do the work of two. And there were tonsils, adenoids, and the appendix, which often grew back if they were not watched properly and nipped, so to speak, in the bud. It was her operation that was making her jittery. How could she be sure that her insides wouldn't grow back when so many other things grew back?

Nature was hard to understand. You clip grass and trim bushes and pluck hairs and what do you get? More grass, stray branches and bushy eyebrows. Miss Ball found that she could not cope with nature. Nature was always ahead of her, ahead of everyone she knew.

Miss Ball had been a farm girl. She could remember seeing her father pushing whole barrows of nourishing dung across rotting boards to the fields. She had peeled potatoes, she had awakened in a musty room covered with a damp quilt. That's how it was when you lived close to the ground. It was damp and you were always kicking plants and dirt back into place, sifting stones, building walls, rocking on the porch and watching the crops fail. This was where Miss Ball learned Mother Nature's spiteful ways.

But her operation had cost her a pretty penny and now, with her childhood thoughts of crabgrass and her recent discovery that lungs ballooned and adenoids reappeared, and—most discouraging of all—that Juan had been extremely, shall we say, virile, and now was dead, Miss Ball could not remember if the doctor had given her a warranty.

She had gotten one with her Snooz-Alarm—it was a big green-edged one-year warranty that looked like a savings bond. And she had gotten one with her hair dryer, her mixer, her vibrator and her juicer. If anything went wrong she didn't have to raise a fuss. She just told the clerk that it was not in working order and she would get a new one, a new dryer or juicer. But she hadn't got a warranty from the doctor.

She had asked herself many times if she needed one and had always decided no. But she had not yet realized her power over men. She had thought she was too old for that sort of thing. She could always reassure herself that Juan was doing it for the money. Was she too old? Harold Potts didn't think so. And that's finally what scared her.

"You look marvellous!" the doctor said with professional enthusiasm as Miss Ball seated herself on the other side of the desk.

"That's the outside you're looking at. It's the inside I'm worried about."

"There's not much left to worry about," the doctor said. He was going to say ha-ha, but he changed his mind when he saw the expression on Miss Ball's face. He decided to reassure her. "What I mean is, you're empty. So why worry?"

"Empty? That doesn't sound too medical to me."

"I try to simplify things for my patients."

"I'm not stupid, doctor. You can talk plain to me."

"I'm talking plain, Miss Ball. Now what's wrong?"

"I want a warranty and I want it now."

"A what?"

"A warranty. I haven't had a wink of sleep for the past two days. All I could think of was my things, the things you say you removed, only God knows whether you did or not."

"Miss Ball, I'm a medical doctor. I have taken the Hippocratic Oath. Every doctor takes it—it's part of being a doctor."

"I'll take your word for it," Miss Ball snapped.

"About the guarantee . . ."

"Warranty."

"As far as the warranty goes. Why, I can't imagine why you'd want something like that."

"I have one for my radio, my juicer and everything else." Miss Ball laughed helplessly, hollowly, for no reason at all. "I was foolish to have the operation without getting it warranteed."

"You want it warranteed, is that it? That's why you came here today—so I could swear out a warranty?"

"You could have been taking me for a ride."

"A *ride?*" The doctor aimed the top of his head at Miss Ball. "Do you know what you're saying, Miss Ball? Now you're talking about ethics. Yes you are. You're talking about my ethics!"

"How's a body supposed to know what's going on? You come into the room and stab me with a needle. I fall flat and then you fiddle around for three hours . . ."

"Fiddle around? I take you for a ride to fiddle around, and for this you want a warranty?"

"You know what I mean."

"I'm a very busy man."

"I lived on a farm, don't worry."

"Why should I worry about you living on a farm?"

"Sure," was all Miss Ball said.

"I want to assure you that I operated on you. I did my level best, as I do with each and every patient. I have not hounded you for the money."

"You can whistle and wait, for all I care."

"I have nothing but your health in mind."

"Don't worry, I've seen things grow back—grass, eyebrows, adenoids. I've seen things go wrong—my toaster, my dryer, my mixer . . ."

"That's a doctor's business—health. We don't try to frighten patients. We are very busy men."

"Busy my foot. You think you're special, you doctors. That's the trouble with you—you think you're *better* than other people that have to work for a living. You wouldn't know about that, would you? Hard work! Hah! Ever get your hands dirty, real dirty and filthy with hard work?"

"Not that I remember, Miss Ball. I couldn't call myself a doctor if I went around getting . . ."

"And you call yourself a man! Ever wheel a whole barrow of cow manure up a plank? Bet you think it's easy!"

"I never said that wheeling cow manure was easy. It's probably very hard work."

"Probably," said Miss Ball in the same tone of voice.

The doctor asked Miss Ball if she thought he was a quack. "You think I'm a quack, don't you?" he asked.

"Who cares what I think. No one cares."

"I care, Miss Ball. I care a great deal what you think," the doctor said softly.

"All right, I think you're a quack," said Miss Ball.

The doctor bit his lip. He said he had been a doctor a long time. He had healed a lot of wounds, not all of them physical. He had seen a lot of people come and go.

Things grow, Miss Ball thought. Things kept growing and there was little or nothing you could do to stop them. It was Mother Nature's way of getting even with the human race. Everyone suffered. Nature liked ugliness and suffering. Nature wanted fat people and failed crops. Nature wouldn't make you lovely and light. She would keep you fat and fertile. Fertile.

Miss Ball leaned toward the doctor. She almost did not have to act scared. She was scared. But she acted scared just the same, and she shook her head from side to side and up and down, and she said very plainly, "Doctor, I want you to know I'm a very frightened person. I never get a wink of sleep any more."

The doctor reflected and was about to speak. But it was Miss Ball that spoke.

"I think they're growing back, and I want a warranty so they don't."

When all the words reached the doctor he still did not seem to understand what Miss Ball was saying.

"You think *what* are growing back?"

"My things."

"You mean your fallopian tubes?"

"Yes," Miss Ball bit her lip, "those. And the other things you said you took out."

The doctor started to giggle.

"You think it's funny!"

The doctor could not answer.

"You think human suffering and worry is a big laugh!" Miss Ball began to cry, loudly at first, then worked it down to a whimper. Miss Ball sniffed and dabbed at her cheek with a lace hanky. "Cruel. You're a cruel, cruel man."

The doctor apologized. He asked Miss Ball to explain what she meant by the warranty.

After a little hesitation Miss Ball told the whole story. She talked about Mother Nature, about weeds that grew all night and were tall in the morning, about lungs and tonsils, about how she had seen Mother Nature kill her father, about her things—how they would be back as sure as shooting. The least the doctor could do was give her a warranty so they wouldn't grow back. She finished with, ". . . I haven't had a good night's sleep for ages."

The doctor said nothing. He played with his lips for a few moments and stared at the far wall. When Miss Ball thought he was going to laugh once again she started to unfold her hanky. The doctor swiveled his chair back at her and said in a low voice, "I think I understand."

"What about it?"

"I'll do anything you say."

"I want you to warranty the operation."

"I'll do it," said the doctor. He took out a piece of paper and wrote on it.

"Make it a five-year warranty, like my juicer. Five years is good enough. I'll be satisfied."

"No, I won't hear of it, Miss Ball. I'll give you a lifetime warranty for that operation of yours."

"A *lifetime warranty!* Good God," said Miss Ball. Her mouth hung open. She could not find the words to express her thanks. Just when he seemed about the biggest quack she had ever seen he reached into his skinny heart and came up with a lifetime warranty. It was almost too much to ask. "Golly," she finally said, "that's the nicest thing anyone ever did for me."

The doctor handed Miss Ball the piece of paper. He said he had done nothing. Miss Ball protested, and felt like throwing herself at his feet.

On the way out of the office Miss Ball's heart was full of love and life. It pulsed. She felt it thumping there under her brooch and lace like a giant Snooz-Alarm. She was a new woman. Mother Nature could do her worst, could twist nice little tissues into ugly old organs. What did it matter? The wonderful warranty was right there in her handbag.

"When God closes a door he opens a window," Miss Ball murmured over and over again as she walked home to find out what success Mr. Gibbon and Mrs. Gneiss had had with their looking around the Mount Holly Trust Company. Personally, Miss Ball felt she could rob a thousand banks single-handed.

13

"It's all set," Mr. Gibbon said. He and Mrs. Gneiss had found out many valuable things. They knew exactly where the vault was (it was, as a matter of fact, in full view of all the bank customers, as most vaults are) and they had plotted what movements they would make. It would be an elaborate "quarterback sneak:" the women would be standing by, Mr. Gibbon would sneak in with his gun drawn, wearing a disguise. The women would be dressed in very ordinary clothes ("Oh, gee!" Miss Ball said, and slapped the table), and would arrive early at the bank. Everyone agreed that it was a nifty little plan.

The suitcases were next on the agenda. The bodies—or the parts of the bodies—had started making a terrific reek. It was an ungodly odor, Mr. Gibbon said, and then he began telling the two ladies about how trenches smelled exactly like that—and you had to sleep, eat, load your gun and shine your brass right in the thick of it. You could cut it with a knife, in case anyone was interested.

Miss Ball said that, for goodness sake, it must have been just like what Herbie was putting up with at that very moment! The thought of the decaying limbs and trunks of the two communists in the suitcases upstairs made them all feel quite close to Herbie.

"It kind of makes you stop and think, doesn't it?" said Mrs. Gneiss.

They all stopped, sniffed at the smell that had now penetrated right down into the dining room, and agreed. It was as if Herbie was in the next room.

But what to do with those suitcases? Miss Ball suggested burying them. Mr. Gibbon suggested that they should put them, for practical reasons, into lockers at the bus terminal. Why? Because after the robbery, as they were carried on the shoulders of a screaming mob of grateful patriots, they would ask to be taken to the bus terminal. In full view of the mob and nationwide television they would produce the key and throw the locker open, expose its un-American contents to the mayor; they would exchange the locker key for the key to the city of Mount Holly.

Miss Ball called a taxi. The taxi driver was a bit under the weather.

"Nice to see *some* people get a chance to go away," he muttered.

"Oh, *we're* not going *any*where!" Miss Ball chirped.

Mrs. Gneiss was given the task of depositing the suitcases into the lockers. Mr. Gibbon had carefully estimated how much it would cost. He gave Mrs. Gneiss two warm dimes when they arrived at the bus terminal, and called a porter to help. "Give the little woman a hand," he said. "I'll be right back." He winked at Miss Ball.

They should not be seen together in public, it was decided. There was no telling who might be spying on them. Mr. Gibbon said that it was a favorite trick of spies to let you go on with your activities and then nab you at the least likely moment, red-handed, with the goods.

"Well, you just leave the goods to me," Mrs. Gneiss said. Mr. Gibbon and Miss Ball went their separate ways after whispering that they would meet back at the "hideout," as Miss Ball's white-frame house, ringed by nasturtiums, came to be called.

Mrs. Gneiss carried one suitcase, the porter carried the other, heavier one. The porter remarked that it felt as if it were filled with burglar tools.

The moment Mrs. Gneiss lifted the suitcase she knew she had Juan. She felt her nice porous skin turn to gooseflesh as she hurried toward the steel lockers.

"They'll fit right fine in this one," the porter said as he groaned and heaved his big suitcase before a row of big lockers.

Mrs. Gneiss looked at the sign and sighed. DEPOSIT ONE QUARTER ONLY, read a sign over a chromium tongue with a quarter-sized circle punched into it. The tongue seemed to be sticking right at Mrs. Gneiss. She examined the two dimes in her palm and said to the porter, "You got anything more reasonable?"

The porter said that at the other end of the terminal there were some cheaper ones, a little cheesier than these.

"Let's have a look," Mrs. Gneiss said.

They hefted the suitcases once again. Halfway across the floor, near the benches for the waiting passengers, Mrs. Gneiss heard someone say, "What's a lady like you lugging a big suitcase like that all by your lonesome?"

The porter ignored the voice and went on ahead.

Mrs. Gneiss turned. A sailor stood before her. He was wearing a seaman's uniform: the white inverted sand-pail hat, wide trousers, and a tight shirt. He had tattoos on his hairy forearms. He should have been young. It was the sort of uniform young sailors wear. But he wasn't young. He was about fifty, and his potbelly pressed against his sailor shirt. He looked jolly. He lifted Mrs. Gneiss's meaty hand off the handle and hoisted the suitcase. He asked Mrs. Gneiss if she had burglar tools in it.

He alone laughed at his joke. He asked Mrs. Gneiss where she was going. He said that he was going to Minneapolis. Mrs. Gneiss said that she was going to the lockers at the other end of the terminal. This sent the old salt into gales of laughter.

"I hope you don't mind doing this," Mrs. Gneiss said, trying to get an impish smile on her fat face. "My Herbie's in the army."

"Don't say?" the sailor said, interested. "Is he stateside?"

"I don't think so. He's in the front lines as far as I know."

The sailor whistled. "What's he wanna do a thing like that fer? Get hissel' hurt that way if he doesn' watch it."

"Not my Herbie," said Mrs. Gneiss. It hadn't dawned on her that Herbie would get hurt. Now, as she said *Not my Herbie,* it occurred to her that Herbie might get his little brain blown off. She blotted out the thought and grinned at the sailor.

The porter had walked all the way to the end of the terminal and now was walking back to where Mrs. Gneiss stood with the sailor. He looked peeved. "I been waiting for you for about an hour," he said.

"Don't get yer dander up for nothing," the sailor said.

"Where's my suitcase?" Mrs. Gneiss asked.

"Back there. You think I'm gonna cart that around all day you're nuts," he said.

Mrs. Gneiss told the sailor she was in a big rush. She had to get the suitcases into the locker and go right back home (she almost said "to the hideout").

When they reached the lockers at the other end the porter held his mouth open in astonishment. "'At's funny," he finally said. "I coulda sworn I left the thing right here . . ."

Mrs. Gneiss wrinkled up her nose. She did not think it was a great loss. The body that was in the suitcase was not only dismembered—it was dead as well. She was, after all, trying to get rid of it. "Someone must have filched it," she said simply.

The sailor suddenly let loose a wild hoot. He seized the shrugging porter by the shirt and began beating him with his free hand. "Now look what you've gone and done!" he puffed. He shoved the porter up against the lockers with a clang and screamed, "Look what you're making me do!"

Mrs. Gneiss stood quietly and watched. She knew that the sailor would soon get it out of his system. A policeman came by and asked what was going on.

The sailor stopped beating the porter. He was out of breath and could not speak. He shook the porter in the policeman's face.

Mrs. Gneiss explained what had happened. She finished by saying, "I don't see what all the fuss is about. There was nothing very valuable in it."

"Valuable or not," the policeman said, "we don't like this sort of thing happening in Mount Holly. Now you just sit tight and I'll round up that suitcase of yours in a jiffy. The culprit couldn't be far away." He asked for a description of the suitcase and its contents.

Mrs. Gneiss said that it was old, brownish-greenish, and had some personal effects locked in it.

The policeman deputized the sailor and the porter. The three ran out the back door of the bus terminal in search of the suitcase.

Mrs. Gneiss quietly placed the small suitcase (Juan) in a dime-locker and went into the bus terminal Koffee Shoppe and swilled down a huge hot-fudge sundae.

Less than ten minutes later the policeman was back with a rat-faced little bum in one hand and the suitcase (Harold Potts, Jr) in the other. The policeman handcuffed the bum to a post and joined Mrs. Gneiss in another sundae. Afterward, he insisted on having his picture taken with Mrs. Gneiss: he presenting the lost suitcase to her, she thanking him. It took an hour for the press photographer to arrive, but finally Mrs. Gneiss got the second suitcase into the locker. The policeman did the heaving and pushing. He remarked as he was doing it that the suitcase felt as if it were filled with burglar tools.

The sailor and the porter were nowhere to be seen. They were, presumably, still looking for the thief.

"I think I'll just toddle off," Mrs. Gneiss said.

The policeman wouldn't hear of it. He said he'd give her a lift in the squad car. His pal didn't mind. They were both tired of passing out parking tickets. "The jig's up," Mr. Gibbon said, when he saw the police squad car arrive with Mrs. Gneiss in the backseat.

"Gosh, the police!" Miss Ball said. She skipped into the kitchen and slammed the door.

Mr. Gibbon pulled out his pistol and flattened himself against the wall behind the front door.

". . . But just for a sec," the policeman said as he entered. "Gotta get back to the station house."

Mr. Gibbon had carefully unloaded his pistol. Now, as the policeman shuffled in and closed the door, he raised the pistol and brought it down on the top part of the policeman's cap where the bulge of his head showed through. Mr. Gibbon had expected a bone-flaking crunch. There was not a sound like that. Instead there was a soft *splok* and the policeman slumped to the floor.

"Charlie!" Mrs. Gneiss said.

"Rope!" Mr. Gibbon hissed.

Mrs. Gneiss looked at the policeman lying spread-eagled on the floor grinning up at her. "You killed the cop, Charlie, and for no good reason at all, you know that?"

"Get some rope, Mrs. Gneiss, and stop sassing me!"

Mrs. Gneiss rummaged through her knitting basket looking for rope. She sighed and mumbled, "I thought it was a bank we were after . . ."

Mr. Gibbon peeked out the little window at the top of the door and spied another policeman in the car. He yelled for Miss Ball.

The kitchen door opened a crack. "Is it okay to come out?"

"Sure, sure," Mr. Gibbon said.

Miss Ball clapped her hand to her mouth when she saw the policeman on the floor. Her eyes popped over the top of her hand. Mr. Gibbon leaped in back of her and started to tickle her. On the left side he tickled and held her fast; on the right—where most of the tickling was done—he used his pistol. He slipped the ice-cold gun barrel under her blouse and scrubbed her kidneys with it.

"Stooooop! Paaaalllleeeeeeeeeze! Stoooooop it! You're awful, Charlie Gibbon! Stooooo . . ."

Her glee found its way through the door and down the walk, past the nasturtiums and into the front seat of the squad car where another policeman sat reading a magazine.

The policeman blew and whistled, fumbled with the magazine, glanced toward the door, shifted in his seat, and then got out of the car, adjusted his tie in the side-window and hurried up the walk.

* * *

During the night another policeman came and asked Mrs. Gneiss if she had seen the two policemen. He described them and gave her the license number of the squad car.

Mrs. Gneiss said yes, indeed, she had seen those nice policemen—they had given her a lift home. But they couldn't stay, they said. They drove off in the direction of Holly Junction to give parking tickets.

When the inquiring policeman returned to his car his partner asked him what he had found out.

"Nothing," was the answer, "just a nice old lady that doesn't know a thing."

Mr. Gibbon saw the car leave as he sat upstairs in the darkness and looked through a slit in the curtains. He waited a half-hour and tiptoed out of the house to check the squad car that he had driven around back and covered with lilac branches and heavy canvas.

As he sneaked through the nasturtiums he heard, "Hey, you!" Mr. Gibbon froze. He did not move a muscle, did not even brush at a fly that was strafing his wedge-shaped head. He had forgotten his pistol.

A uniformed man came up to him and tapped him on the shoulder.

Mr. Gibbon thought of kneeing the uniformed man and making a run for it. But he knew he didn't have a chance. He started to say something when the man spoke.

"Lady by the name of Gneiss live here?"

"Who wants to know?" asked Mr. Gibbon, finding his tongue.

"Western Union. Got a telegram for her."

It might be a trick, thought Mr. Gibbon. "I'll take it. She's inside."

"Okay, okay. As long as she lives here. Just sign the book."

Mr. Gibbon made every effort to write illegibly in the book. He took the envelope and stayed in the nasturtiums while the Western Union man walked away, glancing back at intervals until he was out of sight.

The car had not been touched. Mr. Gibbon put some more branches on it and then went in the house and gave the telegram to Mrs. Gneiss.

Mrs. Gneiss opened it and read it. When she was through reading it she reached across the table, took a handful of cream-filled chocolates and put them in her mouth. Her mouth bulged and juice ran from the corners of her mouth.

She chewed and did not stop chewing until the whole box of cream-filled chocolates was empty. And when it was, and she looked worried, she handed the telegram to Mr. Gibbon.

REGRET TO INFORM YOU OF YOUR SONS DEATH STOP
KILLED GALLANTLY IN ACTION TODAY STOP GAVE HIS

LIFE FOR HIS COUNTRY STOP THAT OTHERS MAY LIVE
STOP DEEPEST SYMPATHY STOP PERSONAL. EFFECTS FOR-
WARDED FIRST CLASS MAIL TO NEW ADDRESS MOUNT
HOLLY.

14

Dressed in authentic policeman's garb, Mr. Gibbon and Miss Ball stood before the full-length mirror in the hall. Miss Ball had insisted on "being a policeman." It took nearly the entire night to alter the jacket and trousers, but by morning—and a beautiful morning it was, the sun shining, the nasturtiums about ready to burst and bleed they were so full of color and sun—she was finished, and just in time for the robbery.

"We're *cops*!" Miss Ball said. "How I wish my kindergarten could see me!" She brushed the sleeve and adjusted the cap and said, "Isn't it a humdinger?"

Mr. Gibbon straightened Miss Ball's tie and said, "Get them shoes shined and make it snappy, sojer."

Mr. Gibbon had never felt more patriotic. He turned on the radio hoping for the Anthem. The news was on. ". . . Tomorrow will be a national holiday in memory of our boys who have given their lives to preserve our way of life at home and abroad, said the president yesterday. The president is now up and around. He brushed his teeth while sitting on the side of his bed this morning and received scores of well-wishing messages from a host of world leaders. He has also been showered with dozens of floral arrangements and directed that some of them be sent to the front lines to remind the soldiers that the country was with them all the way. This morning, with the help of doctors and nurses, he signed his first piece of legislation. Now for the local news. Mount Holly will celebrate tomorrow with a parade through the business districts. Wreaths will be placed and Troop 45 of the Mount Holly Boy Scouts will carry flags. All are welcome to . . ."

"A holiday tomorrow and all on account of Herbie!" Mrs. Gneiss said. "I knew he had it in him! And isn't that thoughtful of the president?"

"We're gonna march, by God!" said Mr. Gibbon.

"You're darn tootin' we are," Miss Ball said.

And then they remembered that it was Friday, a working day. Mr. Gibbon called Kant-Brake and said he was in sick bay. Miss Ball called the school committee and said she was feeling sluggish and headachey. "A white lie never hurt a soul," said Miss Ball.

A last check of the two tied-up and gagged (and nearly naked) policemen in the cellar showed one to be still unconscious from the conk on the head the day before. The other was hopping up and down, struggling to get free. He was stooped over because of the high-backed chair Mr. Gibbon had tied him to.

"You worried about your pal?" Mr. Gibbon said to the hopping man.

The man continued to hop, trying to get loose. Mr. Gibbon took this hopping up and down for a "yes." "Don't you worry a bit, he'll be fit as a fiddle in a day or two," Mr. Gibbon said heartily.

Then Mr. Gibbon pulled out his pistol. The hopping man's eyes bugged out when they lighted on the pistol. Mr. Gibbon tossed his head in a I-know-what's-best manner and said, "You'll thank me for this someday." He bopped the man on the head.

When Mr. Gibbon came upstairs he said it was zero hour.

"Those two nice policemen are going to catch a death in their undies. It's mighty chilly in that cellar," said Miss Ball.

Mr. Gibbon told Miss Ball to stop worrying her head about little things. There was a country at stake. He went around back, threw off the lilac branches and the canvas from the car, and then proceeded to test each item: the horn, the brakes, the oil, the gas, the siren, the water, and even the windshield wipers. Mrs. Gneiss had told him about TV movie robberies that had failed because the getaway car had run out of gas, or the lights had failed, or it wouldn't start. In one of the movies a man had been gunned down as he pressed the starter and got only an *aw-aw-aw* from the engine. Mr. Gibbon reflected: what is more humiliating than dashing out of a bank after a successful robbery and getting into an ornery car? It must be damned discouraging.

They had started down the street in high spirits when Mr. Gibbon suddenly spun the car around and drove back to the house. He parked around back and said that he'd changed his mind.

"Good," said Mrs. Gneiss. She extracted a handful of jelly beans from her purse and began munching.

"We can't both be policemen," he said, looking at Miss Ball.

Miss Ball started to pout.

"I don't want to spoil anyone's fun," Mr. Gibbon said, calmly. "What I said was, we can't both be policemen. That's all I said."

"But you're the big cheese, Charlie. You can play policeman if you want. Me and Mrs. Gneiss are nothing. You're the one who makes the rules!"

Mr. Gibbon stretched his lips. He was deep in thought. Finally he said, "No, you're right. You be the policeman. But remember to follow orders or I'll give you the business."

"Hot dog!" said Miss Ball. She rolled her eyes and spoofed a face.

136

"Let's get the show on the road," Mrs. Gneiss said, between mouthfuls of jelly beans.

Mr. Gibbon got out of the car and went into the house. He returned dressed in his sneakers ("for quick take-off"), flapping fatigues and wearing a felt hat with the brim turned down all around. He also had a shopping bag with him. He showed the ladies that Old Trusty was inside. He handed both Miss Ball and Mrs. Gneiss police pistols.

He had another idea, he said. He had gotten it as they were driving down the street. He would explain it by and by. They were abandoning the "Quarterback Sneak" plan. They should have scrapped it long ago.

In the meantime he had a few things to do. He made several more trips into the house and came back with some cans of whitewash and a big brush. He looked at the doors. MOUNT HOLLY POLICE was written on the front doors, together with a facsimile of a policeman's badge and the telephone number of the police headquarters. With careful strokes Mr. Gibbon painted the front doors white. Then he removed the large chrome searchlight from the right front fender and the long antenna from the back. These he handed to Miss Ball.

"Give you four seconds to put them back," he said. "Okay, go!"

Miss Ball scrambled to the rear of the car and stuck the antenna in the hole. When she started for the front of the car she glanced back and saw the antenna start to topple—she ran back just in time to save it. But by then she had used up five seconds and still held the chrome searchlight in her hand.

"Criminy sakes," said Miss Ball. "I can't do it for the life of me!" She prepared to pout.

"Now I'm going to show you how to do it proper," said Mr. Gibbon. He whizzed to the back of the car and jammed in the antenna, then huffed to the front fender and, with a little grunt, fixed the searchlight into its socket.

"Think you can do that? Or have I got a real clinker in my platoon?"

After six tries Miss Ball did the same. She managed it in slightly over six seconds. "How's that for an old bag? Clinker indeed!"

Mr. Gibbon stood at some distance from the car and looked at it, closing first one eye and then the other. Finally he took the antenna and searchlight off and put them in the back seat. On the floor of the back he put two buckets of water. A last look at the car, blue and white like a taxi; "Pretty snazzy," he said.

They all squeezed into the front seat, and Mr. Gibbon explained his new plan in detail. He said they should all be shot for not thinking of this plan before. It was surefire. It couldn't miss.

"Oh, botheration!" said Miss Ball. "How can I drive the getaway car if I can't drive?"

Mr. Gibbon told her to pipe down and listen. When he was through talking they synchronized their watches.

It was a little after ten o'clock when Mr. Gibbon drove down Holly Boulevard and turned on to Main Street. Apparently many other people had heard about the holiday and had decided to do their weekend shopping. The traffic was heavy; Mr. Gibbon leaned on his horn and swore.

They had all digested the plan and were impatient to get down to brass tacks. But now the car was stuck at a red light. Mr. Gibbon shut off the engine when he saw no signs of movement in the congestion.

"Tarnation," Mr. Gibbon said. "We'll be here all day in this traffic. Now you can see perfectly well what a godawful headache it must be to run a country. No wonder the president has to have his gall removed. Why, if he didn't he'd be up tightern'a duck's ass from morning to night. Here we are doing our damnedest to help out the country and we're hamstrung from top to bottom with this traffic." He smacked his lips and looked around. "This traffic's thicker'n gumbo."

There was a dark family in the next car. They smiled at Mr. Gibbon. Mr. Gibbon grinned back pleasantly and showed all fifteen of his teeth. He turned to Mrs. Gneiss, who was sitting in the middle. "Don't look now, but there are some You-Know-Whos next door. Hear their radio?" He sighed. "Those spooks sure need their bongo music."

The traffic started again. As soon as the cars began moving Mr. Gibbon shouted, "Did you see the nerve of those bastards? Grinning at me like damn fools. Felt like spitting in their eyes!"

Rage had taken possession of Mr. Gibbon by the time they approached the Mount Holly Trust Company. He was panting, and wetting his lips. He discovered that he could barely speak. He had made it a cardinal rule that everyone should be cool as cucumbers, but Miss Ball (smiling out the window, hoping to catch the eye of one of her hooky-playing kindergarteners who, skipping by, would see their own teacher in her adorable little cop suit) and Mrs. Gneiss (munching dolefully on a Nougat Delite) were the only cool ones in the car.

Mr. Gibbon looked over and said in a tone of voice that neither Miss Ball nor Mrs. Gneiss recognized as Charlie's, "Get that fool hat off! You wanna wreck everything?"

Miss Ball took her hat off and smiled. Mr. Gibbon at that moment developed a facial tic that stayed with him for the rest of his life.

He drove by the bank and then up a side street to the back. Here he pointed the car in the direction of the front of the bank, a little hill, and said, "This is it, boys.

You know what to do." He wrenched his hat down over his ears, and got out of the car and told Mrs. Gneiss to hurry up. Then he felt in his shopping bag for his pistol and started down the little hill which led to the front door of the Mount Holly Trust Company.

Mrs. Gneiss put her Nougat Delite into her purse with her pistol, snapped the purse shut and waddled after Mr. Gibbon.

They entered the bank and went immediately to a side table. Mr. Gibbon put his head down and muttered, "You know what to do."

Mrs. Gneiss ambled to the entrance and stood next to the guard. He wore a brand new uniform and looked rather young. Harold Potts's replacement, thought Mrs. Gneiss. He smiled at Mrs. Gneiss. She smiled back and clutched her purse.

Out back, Miss Ball checked her watch. She stared at it for a full minute, and then took the antenna, the searchlight and the two buckets of water from the back seat. These she put some distance from the car in a little pile together with her policeman's hat. She walked about twenty-five feet away from the pile, which was now between her and the car. She checked her watch again and smiled. Keep cool, she thought.

Mr. Gibbon walked toward the teller's cage.

"White folks move aside," he said.

There were some protests. "Aw, let the old coot have his own way," someone grumbled.

Mr. Gibbon looked hard at the teller and said, "Okay, hand over the money."

The man behind the counter cocked his head and then smiled, "Have you filled out a withdrawal slip, sir?"

Mr. Gibbon put his face up against the bars of the teller's cage so that his nose and chin stuck through. "Hand over the money, all of it, you hear? This is a stickup."

"Beg pardon?"

"A stickup," said Mr. Gibbon. "You're being stuckup. By me. Understand?"

"Perhaps you'd like to have a word with the manager," the teller said.

Miss Ball checked her watch again. It was almost time. She edged over to the pile of equipment, the hat, the light, the bucket. A man appeared next to her. "Got a fare?" he asked. Miss Ball smiled, but did not answer. The man got into the back of the car and opened his newspaper.

Mrs. Gneiss sneaked a look at Harold Potts's replacement and felt in her purse. As soon as she did so Harold Potts's replacement looked inside, almost involuntarily. Mrs. Gneiss quickly took out her Nougat Delite and, grinning, offered him some. "Much obliged," he said, "but no thanks."

"This is the last time I'm gonna tell you. *This is a stickup, now hand over the cash!*"

The people who had been in line in back of Mr. Gibbon started backing away. They looked at him with the kind of nervous puzzlement that arrives as a smirk. The smirks vanished when Mr. Gibbon pulled Old Trusty from his shopping bag and flashed it around. Some people started for the door, but Mrs. Gneiss stepped away from the guard and took aim with her Nougat Delite. "Don't move," she said.

She heard laughter, and then she heard very plainly, "Just a couple of old cranks. Might as well humor them—they don't mean any harm. Just two old farts."

Mrs. Gneiss dropped her Nougat Delite into her purse and yanked out the policeman's .38 caliber Colt, looked for the source of the voice, and dropped him in his tracks with one shot.

She waved Harold Potts's replacement away from the door and gestured for the people to back up against the wall.

Oddly, the moment Mrs. Gneiss fired her gun everyone in the bank raised their arms over their head; even the girls sitting at typewriters many feet away did so. All talking ceased. Just like on television, thought Mrs. Gneiss.

Mr. Gibbon pushed his shopping bag over the counter to the teller. The teller stuffed it with big bundles of money wrapped with paper bands and gave the bulging sack back to him.

At this moment a little brown man shuffled around front and, with his hands high above his head, said, "Don't anyone panic. Just do what the man says. We're insured against theft."

Perhaps out of fear, perhaps out of the rock-hard heroism that is smack in the belly of every good bank manager, the little brown man smiled and nodded obligingly to Mr. Gibbon.

Mr. Gibbon sucked in air and snarled, "I don't want any of your cheap lip!" And he shot the little brown man dead. Like a toy the man gurgled, flapped his dry little hands and went down.

The people in the bank straightened their arms and held them higher.

It was time. Miss Ball picked up a bucket of water and splashed it against the left front door of the car. MOUNT HOLLY POLICE complete with telephone number and badge appeared from under the running whitewash. She did the same with the right front, and on this trip around the car popped the antenna and the searchlight in place. Then she snatched the hat and put it on, pushed up the knot of her tie, got into the car, released the brake, flicked on the siren and started rolling down the little hill to the front of the bank.

The man in the backseat did not look up. He said, "Oak Street," and kept on with his paper.

Mr. Gibbon was standing next to a huge pile of bills when Miss Ball pushed through the door and said with stage gruffness, "Okay, don't anyone move. Drop your guns and get your hands up."

With a clang the guns hit the marble floor of the Mount Holly Trust Company.

"What happened to *him?*" asked Miss Ball, gesturing toward the little brown bank manager curled up in his own blood.

"I didn't *mean* to do it," said Mr. Gibbon.

"Tell that to his widow," Miss Ball said, in a good imitation of Broderick Crawford. She motioned for Mr. Gibbon and Mrs. Gneiss to move on. "Take the money," she said to Harold Potts's replacement. "We'll need it for evidence."

Harold Potts's replacement put the stack of money in the backseat and then got in to guard Mr. Gibbon. The man with the newspaper murmured and made room. Mrs. Gneiss got in front.

Miss Ball released the emergency brake, flicked on the siren again and, as Mr. Gibbon said "Easy does it," the car began rolling faster and faster and then coasting at a good rate away from the bank and down the long slope which gave the little burg of Mount Holly its name.

Epilogue

There is a painting called *The Spirit of '76* (but better known as "Yankee Doodle") that hangs in the Town Fathers' meeting-room in Abbot Hall in Marblehead, Massachusetts. It is well known throughout the length and breadth of the United States. The thought of this picture alone is enough to reduce your average American to helpless saluting.

This painting, executed by A. M. Willard, depicts a battlefield strewn with the rubbish of war, a broken wagon-wheel, some pieces of charred skin, a blackened keg. The sky churns with the fresh soot of recently exploded bombs. In the midst of all this rubbish are three figures marching abreast: a sturdy fellow, his head swathed in a bloody bandage, his lips pursed on a flute, marches on the right; a clean little boy in a blue tri-corner hat and beating a drum struts on the left. In the center, wearing a remarkably clean shirt, his head a riot of white hair, a very old man marches. He is prognathic and he is tapping a big drum. At the lower right a wounded soldier raises his trunk out of the quagmire to wave his filthy cap at the musicians and the tattered flag seen fluttering just beyond their heads.

Although nearly three thousand miles from Marblehead, the citizens of Mount Holly know this painting well. And so it was no accident that the day after the robbery of the Mount Holly Trust Company, in what came to be known as "Herbie's Parade," Mrs. Gneiss, Miss Ball, and Mr. Gibbon, marching right, left, and center respectively (Mrs. G. with her head bandaged) and carrying two drums and a flute, and all of them dressed the part, strode through the streets of Mount Holly. It was their wish. Unlike the trio in the famous painting, they did not march in step, for clasped firmly around their ankles were leg-irons. And although it was something they had not bargained on, they had to play their tunes to the clink of their dragging chains.